ANIMAL
ALERT

LIVING PROOF

Jenny Oldfield

Hodder
Children's
Books

a division of Hodder Headline plc

Special thanks to Julie Briggs of the RSPCA. Thanks also to David Brown and Margaret Marks of Leeds RSPCA Animal Home and Clinic, and to Raj Duggal M.V.Sc., M.R.C.V.S. and Louise Kinvig B.V.M.S., M.R.C.V.S.

First published in Great Britain in 1998
by Hodder Children's Books

1 3 5 7 9 10 8 6 4 2

British Library Cataloguing in Publication Data
A record for this book is available from the British Library

ISBN 0 340 70874 3

Typeset by Avon Dataset Ltd, Bidford-on-Avon, Warks

Printed and bound in Great Britain by
Mackays of Chatham plc, Chatham, Kent

Hodder Children's Books
a division of Hodder Headline plc
338 Euston Road
London NW1 3BH

Foreword

*Tess, my eight-year-old border collie, has been injured
by a speeding car. I rush her to the vet's. The doors
of the operating theatre swing open, a glimpse of
bright lights and gleaming instrument, then, 'Don't
worry, we'll do everything we can for her,' a kind
nurse promises, shepherding me away . . .*

Road traffic accidents, stray dogs, sad cases of cruelty
and neglect: spend a day in any busy city surgery
and watch the vets and nurses make their vital, split-
second decisions. If, like me, you've ever owned or
longed to own an animal, you'll admire as much as I
do the work of these dedicated people. And you'll
know from experience exactly what the owners in
my *Animal Alert* stories are going through. Luckily
for me, Tess came safely through her operation, but
endings aren't always so happy . . .

Jenny Oldfield
19 March 1997

1

'Carly, could you bring the bull-terrier in for premed, please!' Paul Grey's voice came over the intercom into the reception room at Beech Hill Rescue Centre.

Carly jotted an appointment in the diary. 'Sorry, I've got to go,' she told Bupinda. The receptionist was going to have to cope single-handed with the Saturday morning rush of patients. In the crowded waiting room there was the usual mixture of cats with cut paws and dogs with high temperatures, itchy ears or sore teeth.

'That's OK. Thanks for your help.' Bupinda took over, calm and friendly as always. Carly's dad always said that, without Bupinda holding the fort at the front desk, Beech Hill would collapse into chaos. 'Mrs Church and Bertie!' She called out now for a long-haired black cat and his owner to come forward to treatment room number two.

So Carly sped off down the corridor to the kennels at the back of the Rescue Centre. It was a chilly October day. The wind and rain gusted against the windows, while dead leaves whipped and whirled around the exercise yard. She was glad to be inside the bustling, hygienic surgery; part of the fast pace of life at Beech Hill.

'Come on, Sam!' She unlocked the bull-terrier's kennel and coaxed him out.

He limped after her on his badly overgrown dew-claws that had curled under and dug into the skin on the insides of both front feet. Now they would have to be removed under an anaesthetic.

'That's a good boy!' She almost smiled at the sad face he made. His little, red-rimmed eyes, set back in his broad white head, blinked up at her, and his pink tongue lolled. She patted him and led him slowly down the corridor to the operating room. 'Now, there's no need to worry,' she told him. 'My dad's done this operation hundreds of times before. You'll be fast asleep and you won't feel a thing!'

She held open the door to the non-sterile procedures room and watched Sam hobble reluctantly in.

'There you are!' Paul Grey lowered his surgical mask and dumped a used pair of gloves into the disposal bin. He wore a green plastic apron over his open-necked checked shirt. He kept this on as he took a new pair of gloves, ready to move on to Sam's case. 'Do you want to help with this one?' he asked Carly, pointing to the row of aprons hanging from hooks on the wall.

She nodded and slipped one on. It came down almost to her feet, covering her jeans. She could have wrapped it round herself twice. Ready in seconds, she offered to lift Sam on to a table.

'This takes two.' Her dad judged the weight of the patient. 'There's over twenty-five kilos of solid muscle here!'

Together they hoisted the dog on to the sterile surface.

Sam looked round at the tubes and trays, the monitor screens and steel instruments. He hung his head and whined.

'Toughen up, Sam.' Paul Grey told the burly, bandy-legged dog not to be a wimp as he gave him his shot of premed. 'Why, I have sissy miniature poodles and Yorkshire terriers go through this with less fuss!'

'What's the premed for?' Carly kept a soothing hand on the dog's broad head as he settled and lay looking up at her with his sad little eyes. Somehow, this blunt-nosed, barrel-chested breed was so ugly it made her like him all the more.

'It's a sedative to quieten him down. This way he'll need less anaesthetic.' The efficient vet in Carly's dad took over from his jokey side. He chose the shaving and clipping instruments he would need to carry out the

4

surgery. 'It's not a long job, so we won't need to give him gas. One quick shot should do.'

He gave the second injection. Soon Sam's eyelids drooped and shut.

'You see how these fifth claws have curved right round?' Paul rearranged the terrier on to his side and showed Carly the painful, inflamed flesh under the long nail. Carefully he shaved away the hair and asked her for the strong clippers. 'It's best if these dew-claws are removed while the dog's still very young,' he explained. 'It would've spared poor Sam this ordeal at least.'

Carly winced as the clippers cut through the tough nail. Of course, Sam didn't feel a thing. 'Will he need antibiotics?' she asked.

Paul nodded as he began work on the second claw. 'To get rid of the inflammation. We'll give him a broad spectrum antibiotic, which should begin to take effect right away. By this time next week, the whole thing should be just a dim and distant memory.'

Carly listened and took everything in. She stored facts in her head, ready for when she was old enough to study as a vet herself, then lined up more questions. 'What's a broad spectrum antibiotic?'

But before her dad could answer, Liz Hutchins, the junior vet at Beech Hill, swung through the door. She checked the list of operations on the white board on the wall, then ticked off Bertie, the black cat. 'I've X-rayed his back left tibia,' she told Paul. 'Mel's developing the plates right now, but I suspect Bertie's been in a fight and got a bad bite, that's all. I'd be surprised if the X-ray shows a fracture.'

'Will he have to stay in overnight?' If so, Carly would get a bed ready in the cats' residential unit on the first floor.

'No, he can go home in an hour if the X-ray's clear.' Liz snapped the top back on the board marker, then grinned at the still unconscious Sam. 'My, he looks like a bit of a bruiser!'

'Don't you believe it.' Paul stood back, waiting for the dog to come round. Sam's tongue slipped sideways out of his mouth and he began to lick his lips. 'He's soft as anything!'

'Don't say that. I like him!' Carly stuck up for the poor bull-terrier. She stroked his thick neck as he opened his eyes and lifted his head.

'Show me an animal you don't like!' When Liz laughed, she wrinkled her nose and her blue eyes nearly closed. 'By the way, Carly, I'm booked in to give a talk at the local meeting of SNAP this afternoon. Do you fancy coming along?'

'What's SNAP?' She was curious about what the young vet might be doing on her official afternoon off.

'It's a bit of a mouthful, but they do important work all over the country. Are you ready for this? It's the Society for Neutering All Pets. SNAP; see?'

Carly nodded. 'What are you going to talk about?'

'They want me to tell their audience what happens at a place like Beech Hill when owners decide not to get their pets spayed and neutered. You know; all the unwanted kittens and puppies without homes. People not knowing what on earth to do when their pet suddenly produces offspring. Sometimes they bring them to the Rescue Centre, of course. But they're the more caring ones.'

'I don't see what's "caring" about owners who can't be bothered to look after their pets properly,' Carly muttered.

'Yes, but you know that more often than not litters will just be dumped by the side of a road, or on a building site, to starve to death.' Liz spoke fiercely as she thought of the people who would do this. Then she explained what SNAP was trying to do about the problem. 'We need to get the right information out and about among the general public: that it doesn't cost much to get your pet neutered; that in certain cases, if you're on benefits, you won't need to pay anything at all. We know people might not have much money, so we want to get that message across.'

Carly nodded. 'Can I go?' she asked her dad.

'You mean, I can't tempt you with an exciting trip to the supermarket?' He told her with a grin about his own plans for the afternoon.

'Yuck, shopping!' She pulled a face and

helped him lift a groggy Sam down from the table. 'Can I, please?'

'Sure. It sounds like a very good cause.' Paul Grey was already looking at the next operation on the list and asking Carly to take Sam back to the kennels in his own good time.

And so Carly and Liz arranged to meet up in reception after surgery was over. Then they plunged on through the case-load: Malibu, a white cat with two broken teeth; Jasmine a kitten with sore eyes; plus an emergency RTA witnessed by a member of the public.

'He's in shock!' Liz took control from Steve Winter, the inspector at the Rescue Centre who'd brought the injured dog in. Steve had carried the spaniel-cross into treatment room two. 'The jaw looks broken, see!'

Carly had rushed in to help. She saw a lot of blood pouring from the dog's mouth.

Gently Liz took off the collar with its metal disc and handed it to her. 'Take the details from there and get Bupinda to ring the owner.'

'The driver didn't stop,' Steve was reporting to Liz as Carly ran to the desk. But the witness

ANIMAL ALERT

took the car registration number. I passed it on to the police.'

Good! Carly thought. She left them to it, shaken by what she'd seen. The little dog had been shivering from head to foot, and lying helpless on a special stretcher that Steve carried in his van. She hoped that the car driver would be made to pay.

'He's called James.' In reception, Bupinda took the dog's collar and read the name on the metal disc. She jotted down the phone number and prepared herself to pass on the bad news to the owner.

Then Steve came out with the stretcher and told Carly that there was more work to do. 'Come with me!' he said, as he dashed through the waiting room out of the main doors into the carpark.

She ran after him in the rain. 'How's the RTA?'

'Liz has stopped the bleeding. She's going to keep him in intensive care overnight and X-ray him tomorrow ... if he gets that far.' Steve's face was grim as he opened up the back

10

door of the Beech Hill van and stowed the stretcher. 'But look what else we have here!'

Carly peered into the van. She gasped when she saw a large pet carrier crowded out with a mother dog and five pups. 'What's wrong with them?' she cried.

'Nothing.' Steve edged the carrier towards the doors. 'Meet Peggy. She's the mum.'

Peggy was a mixture of all sorts. Part-corgi, part-Border collie by the look of her stumpy legs and bushy tail. Her puppies were all colours: black, brown and fawn, with long, silky hair and cute round faces. 'If there's nothing wrong with them, why have you brought them here?' Carly helped Steve lift the carrier into the Rescue Centre.

'Guess,' he said glumly. This had not been a good morning for the inspector.

'The owner doesn't want them any more.'

'Right first time. She called me out to her house on King Edward's Road to take them away. Says she can't cope. She'll call in shortly to sign them over.'

Signing over was a thing that made Carly

partly angry and partly sad. The owner of an unwanted pet had to fill in an Animal Acceptance Agreement giving the reason for parting with the animal and agreeing that the Rescue Centre could go ahead and find a new home. But with Peggy and her pups it would mean a search for *six* new homes. Carly sighed as they took them out of the rain and through to the kennels.

'We'll give them a number each and begin to fill out the forms,' Steve told her above the din of dogs barking and jumping up at their wire doors.

'Do they need feeding?' she asked anxiously, peering into the end kennel where they'd put the new arrivals.

'No. Peggy's still feeding the pups herself. Let her settle in, then we'll feed her as normal this evening.'

They closed the door on the new arrivals and trudged back to reception.

'A busy morning?' Steve noticed that Carly was quiet and dragging her feet. He held the door for her and gave her a kind smile.

She sighed again. 'I don't mind being busy. It's stuff like the RTA and now Peggy that gets me.' Though she'd lived at Beech Hill with her dad since she was four years old, Carly never got used to people's carelessness and cruelty towards animals. *No wonder Liz does her best to get the SNAP message across*, she thought to herself.

'We'll get Peggy neutered as soon as the pups are weaned,' Steve promised. 'And we'll give them all the proper jabs.' He tried to look on the bright side. 'Then, when they're identichipped and ready, we'll start looking for good homes for them. You can help me and Bupinda fill in the AAA forms.'

Carly nodded, going over to Bupinda's desk and picking up one of the forms. She wrote a number at the top of the form, then printed 'Beech Hill' in the box that asked for the name of the centre. In the box marked 'Inspector', she put Steve's name. Then she heard a car draw up outside.

'Go away, we're closed!' Bupinda heard it too.

'Uh-oh!' Carly was the first to spot the blue flashing light on top of the police car. 'What now?'

Forgetting the form-filling, she dropped her pen and ran to the door. A young woman police officer was opening the back door of the car and trying to lift something from the seat. 'I think it's a dog!' Carly gasped.

She couldn't be sure at first because the police officer was stooped over and in the way. And then she couldn't be sure because the animal, whatever it was, looked to be in a very bad state. It lay limp in the officer's arms, long legs dangling, head trailing against her arm. Fear crept into Carly as she stood on the step and the cold rain blew against her.

'Come on, Carly!' Steve Winter jolted her into action. They both ran to help.

'Loose dog!' the police officer told them, her face half-hidden under the brim of her hat. 'Found by a security guard roaming round Ringways Shopping Centre, poor thing!'

Rain soaked straight through Carly's sweat-shirt and trickled down her face. The dog was almost unconscious. It was so thin, every bone in its exhausted body stuck out.

Steve led the way inside. 'It's a greyhound,' he muttered. 'Doesn't look as if it's had anything to eat for days!'

'No collar, no means of identification,' the policewoman reported as she brought the dog in out of the cold wind. 'But it's covered in sores and cuts, and it's absolutely filthy. I wouldn't have believed the state it was in if I hadn't seen it with my own eyes.'

'And no owner around, I presume?' Steve's tone of voice made it clear that he knew he need hardly bother to ask.

'Not a sniff of an owner,' she confirmed.

Carly heard the muttered talk, but hardly took in the details. She watched as the dog was carried into a treatment room and laid on the table. It was skeleton-thin; a brown-and-black brindle colour, but covered in dirt and red sores. As it tried to struggle to its feet, she saw how it could hardly lift its head. Its long tail curved between its legs, its ears were laid flat and the eyes that should have been round and bright were half-closed and dull with pain.

'I take it you'll prosecute if you get anywhere near the owner?' the policewoman asked Steve.

'It's definitely a cruelty case,' he agreed. 'Can we make it a police-assist case?'

She nodded. 'I'll give you all the help I can.' Taking her hat off, she shook the rain from the brim. 'Like I say, it's a question of whether or not we ever manage to track down an owner. Personally, if I had anything to do with this, I'd keep my head well down.'

Still Carly watched the dog struggle to raise herself. She saw each rib in her bruised and battered sides, saw where the bones of the pelvis jutted out square. 'What are you doing?' she cried out to Steve, as the inspector went to a drawer in the cabinet by the window and took out a camera.

He went in close and pointed the lens at the struggling dog. 'Taking photographs of the condition she was in when she arrived,' he told her.

The dog had made it on to her feet. She stood

and trembled, sides heaving, head cowed and hanging low. The camera clicked and whirred.

'Why?' Carly cried again. Why didn't they rush to bring Liz or her dad to help the poor creature?

'Evidence,' he insisted, his face behind the camera lined by a deep frown. Another series of clicks and whirrs as the dog's legs buckled and she collapsed. 'When we bring the case to court, we have to show that the owner has committed a cruelty offence. These photographs should do it.'

'Surely the dog herself is evidence enough?' the policewoman asked, shaking her head sadly.

'Yes!' Carly agreed. Anyone could see that this owner was guilty of terrible cruelty. They had the living proof right here in front of their eyes!

'The point is, the dog might not make it.' Steve finished taking the photographs and put the camera down. 'She might be too far gone for us to help.'

2

'Who could treat an animal this way?' Carly moved closer to the table as the inspector went to fetch one of the vets. She could see raw red sores on the greyhound's back leg and hindquarters, and a patch of fur rubbed bare around her neck. 'It looks like she's been tied up!' She pictured the dog straining at a rough tether until the noose cut through to the flesh. 'Maybe in the end she managed to escape.'

The police officer shrugged. 'Who knows? The only information I have is that one of the security guards spotted her in the shopping centre carpark. She looked like a stray, so he rang us. I don't think anyone realised what a bad state she was in. I mean, greyhounds are always thin, aren't they?'

'But not this thin!' Gently Carly laid a hand on the dog's head as she lay panting from the effort of trying to stand.

'Mind she doesn't turn on you.'

Carly nodded. A dog who had been so badly treated might well turn nasty. But the greyhound only nudged her head slightly towards the soothing hand, as if glad of the kindness.

'OK, let's see what we've got!' Paul Grey came quickly into the treatment room and started giving orders. 'We'll get her through into theatre, shall we? We'll need the resuscitation equipment on stand-by. Carly, run and fetch Mel. Steve, let's wheel her through!'

Suddenly it was all action. Doors swung open and closed, wheels rattled down the corridor, the inspector grabbed a spare apron and hung it round his neck. Carly went for the nurse, who was in the office winding down after a hectic morning. Mel came running with her to the operating theatre, to find the patient already hooked up to a drip.

'This is Hartmann's solution,' Paul told them, as he fixed the syringe into place with tape around the dog's front leg. 'To replace the fluid she must have lost through dehydration, and to help her get over the trauma she's suffering. Mel, stand by with oxygen.'

Carly stood to one side, anxiously watching the experts at work. Next, her dad sounded the dog's chest with his stethoscope and felt for a pulse. He gave a slight shake of his head. 'Irregular and thready,' he muttered. 'I'm wondering if there's some damage to the organs as well as all this superficial bruising.'

'Internal bleeding?' Mel asked. The nurse wheeled the oxygen trolley close to the treatment table.

'It would explain the irregular pulse. But, then again, that could be straightforward shock.' Paul paused to think. 'It doesn't look to me like she'd stand an anaesthetic right now.

That cuts out an exploratory operation, so what we'll do is give her an antibiotic, and leave her to settle down in intensive care for a few hours.'

'But what if she *is* bleeding?' Carly stepped forward. Surely they should be doing more to save the dog. 'Won't it get worse if we leave it?'

'We'll have to take that risk,' her dad told her. 'She's just too weak to do anything with until we stabilise her condition.' He patted her shoulder to show that he understood. 'Trust me, Carly. We'll keep the dog warm and comfortable in intensive care. We'll monitor her heartbeat. Meanwhile, all we can do is wait and hope.'

With the patient safely installed in intensive care, the first crisis was over. The Rescue Centre was quiet and calm, as Carly stood in reception with her dad, the police officer, Steve and Bupinda.

It was half an hour since the starving greyhound had been brought in, and so far there was no sign of any serious internal damage. Carly kept her fingers crossed, waiting for Liz to take her to the talk she was due to give.

Mel had just checked the monitor and joined the others in reception with the latest news that the patient was still holding her own.

'She must have been a beautiful dog once,' the nurse said quietly. 'You can tell from her face that she's a good pedigree specimen. That long narrow head and those big round eyes are classic greyhound.'

'Sight hounds,' Steve Winter told them. He stood with his arms folded, leaning against the wall where photos of rescued and rehoused dogs and cats were pinned up on view. 'Bred originally for pure speed to track down moving prey. These days they're more likely to be seen as the ultimate racing machines. But when their days at the racetrack are over, they make surprisingly good pets: lovely, gentle creatures, very good-natured.'

'Talking of lovely, gentle creatures,' Paul Grey broke in, lightening the mood as usual, 'here come Hoody and Vinny!'

Carly's friend, Jon Hood, was strolling across the rainy carpark. His jacket was unzipped, his faded black T-shirt flapping in the wind. Instead of avoiding the puddles, he ploughed through them, hands in pockets, shoulders hunched and glowering straight ahead.

'I take it you mean Vinny!' Mel laughed.

Vinny, Hoody's tough mongrel dog, was the sensible one at least. He neatly skirted the puddles and headed for the shelter of the entrance porch at a quick trot.

Carly went to open the door for them. But as soon as Hoody spotted the police car tucked away down the side of the building, he froze in mid-stride.

'Wuh! Here, boy!' He called his dog back and swung away in the opposite direction.

So Carly had to run after them and tell him about the cruelty-case dog. 'You know your trouble?' she said, as she dragged them into reception.

'No, but you're gonna tell me.' He stood in the porch and shook his short, wet hair.

'You've got a guilty conscience. Every time

you see the police, you think it's you they're after.'

Hoody peered through the plate glass at the officer in uniform. 'You got that the wrong way round. Every time *they* see me, they think it's *me* they're after!'

She laughed. 'Well, not this time. Unless you've just beaten up and starved a pedigree greyhound and dumped her in Ringways Shopping Centre!'

Hoody hated everything on two legs, especially when they wore uniform. But he liked everything with four legs, and he loved dogs. 'Yeah, right!' he muttered, eager to hear more. 'This greyhound; is she gonna be OK? I mean, your dad's had a look at her, right?'

As they crossed the waiting room to join the small group in reception, Carly told him the details.

' . . . Of course, since there's no dog register these days, it makes the task of tracing the owner all the more difficult,' Paul Grey was saying. 'And this particular animal hasn't been identichipped.'

Carly stopped talking and she and Hoody listened hard.

'If she'd been chipped, we'd have all the information we would need,' Steve explained to the policewoman. 'Name of owner, address and so on. As it is, we don't seem to have any kind of lead whatsoever.'

Putting on her hat, ready to leave, the police officer agreed. 'But we're not just going to let it drop, are we?' She was determined that the police and the Rescue Centre together should do everything they could.

'No.' Steve frowned and chewed his lip. 'This is a bad case. I want us to follow it up, but we need a clue to start us off on the right track. Are you sure there's nothing else you can tell us?'

'Let's see.' She listed the few known facts on her fingers. 'One: the dog was found on one of the upper levels of the multi-storey carpark at Ringways. Two: she can't have been there long because the carpark is manned by security staff and they patrol the place at half-hourly intervals. Three: no one parking their cars reported seeing the dog, and the member of staff in the ticket booth says he's pretty sure no one drove into the carpark with the greyhound in the car. And,' she added finally, 'no one with a dog used the lifts in the hour or so before she was spotted.'

'But she can't have appeared out of nowhere!' Carly protested. 'Someone must have taken her in there!'

For a few seconds there was silence.

'There's a back way in.' Hoody spoke for the first time. All heads turned towards him. 'Well, there is!' he glared back at the police officer. 'I know exactly where it is. If you're on foot, you can use an entrance by the canal. It's sort of poky and dark, so hardly anyone goes that way.'

'That's right.' The woman in uniform narrowed her eyes and went on staring at Hoody. 'It's opposite the pub.'

'The Longboat,' Hoody muttered, then dried up completely. He sniffed and backed off, almost bumping into Liz Hutchins as she came out of the office.

'What time is it?' Liz muttered, flinging on

26

her jacket as she dashed by. She checked the clock on the wall behind Bupinda's desk. 'Half past one! Oh, great, I'm going to be late for my talk! You coming, Carly?' She was already halfway out of the front door.

Carly dashed after her, avoiding Hoody but almost tripping over Vinny in her hurry. 'Do you mind if I don't come?'

'Changed your mind?' Liz made a run through the rain to her parked car.

'Not exactly. Only something's come up. It's important.' She didn't want to leave things with the greyhound hanging in the air as they were right now.

'Cruelty case?' The young vet slid into the driver's seat and paused to look up at Carly. 'I heard about it. Pretty bad, eh?'

She nodded. 'I thought Hoody and I could go and take a look round Ringways to see what we can find out.' The idea had popped into her head as she listened to the police officer's account.

'We can?' Hoody came up behind. 'Like, you asked me first?'

Carly ignored him. Once he thought about it, he would see it made sense. 'I can't see the police giving the case a lot of time, even though they've agreed to help. The officer who brought the greyhound in will have to report everything, and when they see that we don't have any clues to go on they'll say there's not much point, won't they?'

'Maybe.' Liz looked at her watch. 'Good for you, Carly, if you want to have a go. But it won't be easy.'

'I know.' Outwardly Carly sounded confident, but inside she felt scared by the idea of looking for the dog's cruel owner. Having Hoody and Vinny with her would make all the difference. She turned to Hoody as Liz wished them luck and drove off. 'Do you want to see the dog?' she asked.

'What's its name?'

Typical Hoody, to answer a question with another question. 'I take it that means yes?' Carly led the way back inside, passing the police officer on her way out. 'We don't know her name or anything about her. And she's a she, not an it.'

Grumbling and shuffling his feet, Hoody told Vinny to stay in reception and followed Carly into intensive care.

'Are you ready?' she asked in a whisper, holding the door open for him. 'It's really bad, remember!'

He nodded. But he wasn't really prepared. As he strolled forward into the room lined with charts, instrument racks, oxygen cylinders and plastic tubes, and saw the greyhound lying inside a see-through unit, Carly heard him gasp, saw him stiffen.

The dog was sedated and hooked up to the drip. She lay on her side; long, skinny legs stretched straight out, eyes closed. She looked nothing but skin and bones; no flesh to soften the angles of her poor, starving frame. Every rib showed, every breath seemed slow and painful.

'She's covered in sores!' Hoody crept forward for a closer look, noticed the tape round her leg holding the drip in place, saw where Paul and Mel had bandaged and patched her up. 'Who did this?' he hissed.

'Exactly.' The urgency in Carly's voice made Hoody look up. '*Now* will you come to Ringways with me?'

3

Ringways Shopping Centre was on the same side of town as Beech Hill. It was a modern concrete and glass complex with wide ramps and under-cover shops that sold clothes, hi-fis, books and holidays. A huge area of old brick offices had been cleared to make room for it. On one side it overlooked the inner-city ring road and the main town library beyond. On the other, it backed on to the canal.

The back entrance was the one which Carly, Hoody and Vinny made for that Saturday afternoon in the wind and the rain.

'Be careful,' Carly's dad had warned when he heard their plan. 'Steve has to go to another job, so you'll be on your own this afternoon. If you do find out anything about the dog's owners, don't do anything on the spot. Come straight back here so we can pass it on to the police.'

She'd promised to be sensible, but it had taken a back-up promise from Hoody to convince him.

'Don't worry, I'll watch her.'

' . . . Because she tends to jump in with both feet, remember,' Paul Grey had warned. 'Especially where an ill-treated animal is concerned.' He knew his daughter too well.

It had only been because Vinny would be there to keep an eye on things that he'd reluctantly agreed to let them go. Vinny might be a small dog, but he was strong and reliable, and his bark was fierce.

And now, as they stood outside the back entrance to the carpark, Carly was glad they had him with them. He stood guard at the battered blue door as they scanned the back street, legs wide apart, tail up, ears pricked.

Hoody stared up and down the street. He kicked an empty can into the gutter and watched it roll away in the wind. 'What are we waiting for?' he asked.

'Just looking.' Carly took in the narrow, humped bridge over the canal, the road signs that showed this area was for pedestrians only. She read the pub sign opposite – 'The Longboat' – then noticed the empty wooden tables and benches in the courtyard to the side. There was no one in sight in either direction. 'Let's go,' she muttered.

So they climbed the concrete stairs, trying to ignore the stale smell, counting the levels until they came to the top. Then they pushed open a stiff door into the carpark itself, coming to a halt by a pay-and-display ticket machine.

'What now?' Hoody frowned at the rows of parked cars.

Carly sighed. She was damp and cold. Faced with lines of rain-spattered, deserted cars, she realised for the first time that starting the search here in the carpark was going to be more difficult than she'd imagined. 'The police woman said the dog was found on an upper level,' she insisted grimly.

'But there's no one around to ask!' He wandered aimlessly back into the stairwell and looked down the flights of dirty stairs. 'I think we should work our way down to the level where the shops are and start asking there.'

Without waiting for Carly to agree, Hoody called Vinny and took the steps two at a time. He was three levels down before she decided to follow.

'There's an entrance!' he yelled up. 'With an automatic door. The dog could have come through here!'

'What are we going to ask?' She followed him down and stepped after him and Vinny into the brightly lit, warm, dry shopping area. There was piped music, neon signs, people everywhere.

'You mean, *who* are we going to ask?' Suddenly Hoody was less sure. 'How many hours is it since this all happened?'

'About two.' She knew what he meant: none of these busy shoppers would have been around when the police picked up the loose dog. 'Let's try in the shops opposite,' she suggested. 'Maybe the people working there would have seen something.'

'Split up. I'll go into the music shop, you go into the clothes shop.' Hoody's idea was that they would get more information this way.

'Just because you won't set foot inside a shop that sells dresses!' she muttered. She had to steel her nerves to go in alone.

'Yes?' The girl serving at the till came out from behind her desk. She'd quickly spotted Carly.

'Erm, we . . . I was wondering, did you see a stray dog round here?' Weird question inside this carpeted, clean and shiny space, she knew.

The girl gave her a strange look. 'Oh yeah!'

'No, really. It's a greyhound; sort of brown-and-black stripy. Really thin . . .'

'Is it your dog, then?'

'No.'

'Why are you looking for it?'

'We're not looking for her. We know where she is . . .' The girl's eyebrows had shot up, she was about to call her supervisor, so Carly gave up trying to explain. 'You didn't see her?'

'No! OK?'

She nodded and backed out of the shop, straight into Hoody, who was in retreat from the music shop next door.

'Don't tell me!' Hoody said. 'They acted like you'd gone mad?'

'Right. So?' Carly took a deep breath. The shopping centre wasn't the kind of place where you went around asking unusual questions. It was the kind of place where you went into a shop, tried something on, paid your money and came out again without saying a word.

No one looked you in the face. They hurried along the walkways, ignoring the man playing the guitar by the exit with his guitar case on the floor in front of him to catch spare coins, and his skinny dog sitting beside him . . .

Hoody spotted the busker at the same moment as Carly. He glanced at her, shrugged and walked across to listen to the music. 'Nice dog,' he said at the finish of one long, wailing song.

'Thanks.' The busker glanced at Vinny and nodded. Then he launched into another song.

Carly waited impatiently in the doorway of the nearest shop and watched the shoppers bustle by. Only one or two paused to drop a coin in the collection. Most preferred to ignore the long-haired, scruffy guitar-player with the wailing voice. What was Hoody playing at, she wondered; wasting time listening to the dreary music?

'What is he; some kind of whippet?' he asked the singer casually at the end of the second song.

The dog sat patiently on a cosy, striped blanket. He was a mongrel like Vinny, but thinner, with finer features. His face was long, his short, grey-brown coat covered in darker splodges.

'Whippet- and Dalmatian-cross.' The musician leaned his guitar against the shop window. 'I call him Dot.'

Dot heard his name and wagged his long tail.

'How old?'

'Three and a bit. Don't know exactly. He was a stray when I got him.'

'Where from?' Hoody never wasted words. He bent down to stroke the friendly dog.

'I found him on a skip.' The busker had decided he liked Hoody. He didn't seem to be in a hurry to start his next song. 'When I say "on a skip", I mean, someone had taped him up inside a cardboard box and dumped him there. He was only a few weeks old, so he couldn't get out. I just happened to be passing and I heard him making this pathetic kind of noise . . .'

Fascinated by the story, Carly came forward to join Hoody. She made a fuss of Dot, scratching behind his floppy black ears.

' . . . It was a kind of high whining, over and over. At first I couldn't make out where it was coming from. In the end, I tracked it down to the box on the skip, climbed up and found him in there.'

'And you decided to keep him?' she prompted.

'Well, you have to.' To the busker it was the only choice he could have made. 'Dot's been with me ever since. Never lets me down. Even listens to the songs I play as if he likes 'em. You could say he's my main fan.' He grinned and winked. 'What's the story with your dog?' he asked Hoody.

'Another stray. Name's Vinny. Got him from Carly's place.'

'Who's Carly?'

'Me,' she said, blushing as Hoody cut his own story short as usual.

'She lives at a rescue centre. Nobody wanted Vinny except me.' He paused, sure now that they all had a lot in common. He was working round to the important question. 'Did you happen to see a greyhound stray round here earlier?'

The musician frowned. 'Here in the shopping centre? What time?'

'A couple of hours ago.' It was Carly's turn to break in. 'You'd have noticed her because she was so thin, almost starving to death as a matter of fact. The police brought her in. She's a cruelty case, so we're trying to track down the owner.'

'Wow.' Deciding to take a break, the busker stooped to gather the money he'd earned. 'Sounds bad.'

'It is.' She didn't tell him the worst; that it was still touch and go for the greyhound.

'Well, anyway, I didn't see the dog you're on about . . .' He slipped the money into his pocket and zipped the guitar into its case. Dot stood, stretched and yawned.

Carly let a sigh escape. It wasn't the answer they were looking for.

' . . . Not here in the shopping centre.' The musician stood up straight.

'But you did see her?' Hoody cut in.

He nodded. 'Maybe. But the one I'm thinking of wasn't a stray. It had owners with it.'

'Thin, black and brown, a greyhound?' Hoody repeated the description.

'That's the one. I remember seeing it from a

distance and thinking, "God, what a state". But I wasn't gonna get mixed up with those owners. No way!'

'What were they like?' Carly wanted hard facts. At last they were on to something!

'Man and woman.' Their new friend did his best to recall the details. 'In their twenties. Matching leather-jackets; yeah, that's right!' He nodded as if his memory had suddenly cleared. 'Big motifs on the back of the jackets. Matching motifs; the name of a motorbike, something like that!'

Carly nodded encouragement. 'Anything else? Like, where did you see them?'

'Not in here, like I said. It was down by the canal as I was on my way up to start work. They were going into the pub; The Longboat. Saw them from behind, that's why I remember the jackets. But listen, you say it was just the one dog that gave them the slip?'

Hoody cocked his head sideways. 'Yeah, why?'

'Pity,' the busker said, picking up his guitar and rolling Dot's blanket under his arm. 'I mean, it's a pity the other two couldn't make their getaway at the same time.'

As he set off across the shiny marble floor towards the carpark exit, Hoody and Carly ran after him. Vinny and Dot trotted ahead as they pulled at his arm.

'Wait!' Carly pleaded. 'Are you telling us these owners had three dogs altogether?'

'That's right. All greyhounds. I didn't get a good look, but there were definitely three of them.' He shrugged free. 'If you need me to give evidence or anything, you know where to find me.' He jerked his thumb back towards the shop entrance. 'Every Saturday. Isn't that right, Dot?'

Carly and Hoody hardly heard what he said. They watched him stroll through the automatic doors, guitar case in hand, Dot trotting obediently by his side.

The doors closed silently.

'Two more dogs!' Carly whispered.

'Bad news,' Hoody agreed. 'If they can treat one that badly, I reckon they could do it to the other two as well.'

Vinny sat and whined, wondering what was wrong now.

'Three dogs!' gasped Carly. All in danger. One in intensive care at Beech Hill. And now two more still out there, probably being beaten and starved to within an inch of their lives.

4

'It looks like James is going to make it,' Paul Grey told Carly and Steve Winter next morning.

The spaniel-cross who had been in the collision with the hit-and-run driver had survived the night and was due for X-ray.

'And the police have traced the car registration number,' Steve added. 'The driver's looking at a charge of driving without due care and attention. There are witnesses coming forward, and plenty of proof.' He sounded satisfied that things were working out as they should.

If only it was always so easy, Carly said to herself, thinking of the greyhound in the unit next to James. Instead she concentrated on gently lifting the small grey-and-white mongrel and turning him so that he didn't get pressure sores from lying in one position for too long.

'Cheer up,' her dad told her. 'There's good news on the greyhound too.' He scanned the temperature chart and checked the monitor print-out. 'All the vital signs are stable, I'm glad to say. So it looks like there's no serious internal injury after all.'

She flashed her dad a brief smile and went across to the emaciated patient. 'Good!' she whispered, reaching in to stroke the dog. 'When can we give her her first good meal?'

'Not yet. We'll build it up gradually. Her stomach couldn't take a normal diet straight away.' He came to look over Carly's shoulder. 'The important thing is to keep her fluid level up. She'll get all the potassium and other salts and vitamins from that to start with. Meanwhile the antibiotics we started her on yesterday will deal with the infections in the sores.' He explained carefully how they would treat the case of severe malnutrition.

Carly checked a bandage on the dog's front leg. 'See how long her nails are,' she complained.

'We'll leave that for now,' Paul said. He handed Carly a metal dish filled with warm water and a wad of cotton wool pads. 'But you can have a go at cleaning out her ears. I noticed they were absolutely filthy.'

She was glad to do a practical job and set about gently swabbing the delicate inside surface of the patient's floppy, rose-shaped ears. But her mind drifted as she worked, back to the dismal scene outside the back entrance of the carpark the day before; the empty street, the rain-spattered canal and the deserted pub.

She and Hoody had tried to get further with the clues the busker had given them. They'd hung around for ages to see who went in and out of The Longboat, desperate for a glimpse of two figures with matching leather-jackets. They'd even gone round to the back door and asked to speak to the landlord to see if they could prise any information out of him. But a barman had answered the door, given them one look, shaken his head and roughly told them to clear off.

It would have been too much to hope that the careless, cruel owners of the greyhounds would actually return.

So they'd trailed back miserably to Beech Hill, doubly worried because now they knew that two more dogs were suffering at the hands of the mysterious owners.

'You did well,' Steve had told them when he listened to the new clues. 'We have a description. We know where they might hang out. That's definitely an improvement on what we had before.'

Carly finished cleaning both ears and went to swill the filthy water down the sink. As she looked up, she jumped. Hoody and Vinny had their faces pressed close up against the window, waiting for her to see them. Vinny's hot breath clouded the clear pane. 'You gave me a fright!' she mouthed.

'How's the greyhound?' Hoody mimed the words through the glass.

'Good!' Carly nodded and gave a thumbs-up sign. She gestured towards the main entrance and told him to come round, then went to let him in.

'You gave me a fright!' she told him again as she opened the door.

'The door was locked.' He shrugged and brushed past with Vinny in tow.

'Well, it *is* Sunday!' The Rescue Centre was closed while the others took time off. Today it was Paul and Steve's turn to work. 'Anyway, Dad's just told me that the greyhound should make it.'

Hoody paused and nodded. 'Have you thought of a name for her?'

'No. Why?'

'She should be called something, not just "the greyhound",' he insisted. 'How about Grace?'

Carly agreed. 'I bet she *was* graceful once,

when she got enough to eat.' She pictured the dog's long legs and proud, arched neck galloping at speed.

'And will be again.' Hoody was determined. 'Listen, I'm gonna stake out The Longboat again. Do you want to come?'

She hesitated. It seemed like a long shot. 'Anyway, supposing we do find out more, what will we do then?' She remembered how their busker had told them that even he had backed off from tangling with the leather-jacketed owners of the three mistreated dogs.

'Fetch Steve,' Hoody answered.

'Fetch me to do what?' The inspector himself came out of intensive care into reception. He only needed to listen to the beginning of Hoody's explanation before he was telling them both to hop into the van and wait for him there. 'We'll all drive down-town and take a look,' he insisted. 'If you spotted these characters, there'd be no time to ring me here and for me to drive over. By the time I got there, there'd be nothing and no one to investigate.'

'Are you sure you've got time?' Carly asked.

'It's my job. I'm the strong arm of the law round here!' Steve had trained as an inspector after he'd given up working as a builder a few years earlier. He was patient but firm, good at picking up clues and interviewing owners of animals that had been lost or badly treated. Above all, he cared about the innocent victims of cruelty and neglect.

Carly was glad he would be with them that lunch-time, as they cruised through the empty streets and down underpasses into the city. The rain had eased overnight and a weak sun filtered through the grey clouds.

'Here's the canal.' Hoody pointed out the humped bridge and the pub beyond. Behind them towered the concrete slabs of the multi-storey carpark.

So Steve turned down a side street and parked the van, took off his inspector's jacket to make himself less noticeable, and told Carly and Hoody to lead the way.

'What's the theory?' he asked as they walked over the bridge and paused to glance down at the stretch of brown water and the lock fifty metres down the canal. 'Why did you want to come back here?'

'I reckon The Longboat is their local,' Hoody answered. 'If we stick around long enough, they're bound to come for a drink. And Sunday is a good day.' He pointed out the smattering of people who had braved the autumn weather to sit on the wooden benches outside the pub.

Steve nodded and led the way. 'OK, let's mingle.'

Soon they were sitting with full glasses at one of the outside tables, picking up bits of information from other customers, keeping their eyes peeled.

'We had the police round the estate last night,' an old man at a nearby bench told his neighbour.

'Again?' The middle-aged woman sat hunched inside a red padded jacket, obviously bored.

'Someone rang them about the noise. Didn't you hear the police car pull up outside?'

Carly overheard the slow chat, half paying attention, half her mind on looking for a couple in matching leather-jackets. More customers got out of a car and sauntered into the pub, but they looked nothing like their suspects. In fact, if she was honest, she was beginning to give up hope. Perhaps the friendly busker had made the whole thing up?

'. . . I must have been out when they came. What was it; kids?' The bored woman muttered. Police coming to their housing estate was obviously not big news to her.

'No. It was those flipping dogs,' the old man grumbled. '*Bark-bark-bark*; non-stop! Day in, day out. It gets on your nerves.'

Carly turned to stare at the grumpy speaker. And she tuned in and began to listen hard.

'I blame the Wilsons, not the dogs. It's the way they treat 'em. They tie 'em up and don't give 'em enough exercise. Dogs are bound to kick up a fuss if you leave 'em locked up in a tiny place like that.'

Nudging Steve and Hoody, Carly warned to listen in too.

'Not fit to have dogs, some people . . .' The old man tailed off through lack of encouragement. He cleared his throat then took a sip of beer.

'I never did like the Wilsons,' the woman in red moaned. She wore red lipstick to match her jacket, and her grey hair was scraped back behind a broad red scarf.

'It's all right for you. You don't have to live next to them.'

'Opposite's bad enough. I can still hear the dogs loud and clear. When they got this third one the other week, it was more than I could stand. It's never stopped barking from the day it arrived.'

Just then, Vinny whined. Carly looked down and realised that she was holding him too tight by the collar. It seemed important to keep him hidden under the table until the anti-dog conversation was over. 'Sorry!' she whispered. These Wilsons; who were they? And where did they live with their three noisy dogs? She was convinced that the information was vital.

'Of course, the police didn't do anything,' the

old man went on. 'Just hammered on the door at number 22, and when they got no answer they gave up. I went and told 'em the Wilsons were out at the racetrack, like every Saturday night. That's why the dogs were making a racket. They tie 'em up when they go out and the poor things can hardly move . . .'

Steve, Carly and Hoody had heard enough.

'Number 22?' Carly interrupted. 'Whereabouts is this flat you're talking about, please?'

The man and woman looked sideways at them. 'Who wants to know?' the old man said.

Steve stood up and explained who he was and why they were there. 'We think you can help us. These people; the Wilsons, what's their exact address?'

Carly bit her lip as their informant hesitated.

'Oh, I don't know if I should get involved,' he muttered. 'If they got to hear who'd spilled the beans, they wouldn't be very happy with me.'

'It'll be confidential,' Steve assured him. 'We won't tell a soul.'

There was another pause, while the woman

rummaged in her handbag and the old man cleared his throat once more.

'Of course, I do feel sorry for the dogs,' he admitted. 'It's not right; treating decent, perfectly healthy animals that way, just because their racing days are over.'

'They deserve better,' Steve agreed.

'But, on the other hand, I never like to interfere.'

'I understand that. But, this way no one will ever know.' He was patient, calm, dogged.

'Go on, tell them, why don't you?' the woman urged. 'If you don't, I will.' She snapped her handbag closed and looked Steve in the eye. 'It's Jet and Misty Wilson you're looking for. And they live at number 22 Beacon Heights. It's on the estate behind the ring road. You can't miss it.'

The Wilsons' flat was at the end of a first-floor balcony shared by half a dozen other shabby entrances. Carly's footsteps echoed along the concrete walkway as she kept up with Steve, Hoody and Vinny. Number 16 . . . 18 . . . 20. The next door along was number 22.

'Wait!' Steve put out his arm and barred the way.

Rowdy electric-guitar riffs blasted through the closed door and windows next door. One window was boarded up, the other filthy and strung with a yellowy-grey net curtain. They waited outside number 20 until the amateurish music abruptly stopped.

'Hear that?' Carly gasped.

From inside number 22 they could hear dogs whining and yapping.

'This looks like the right place,' Hoody muttered, anxious to press ahead.

There was a clatter and an electronic hum, the sound of someone carelessly dropping a guitar, then a sharp bark from one of the dogs. A man's voice yelled at it to get out of the way.

'Go on, get out of here! You're asking for it, you are!'

There was a heavy thud, some swearing, and a woman's voice whining and complaining about the noise.

'Come on!' Carly urged. There was more

abuse, and now one of the dogs was yelping with pain. A second one seemed to be bundled up against the front door, frantically scratching to get out.

So Steve drew himself up and went to ring the bell. He listened, heard nothing. 'Broken,' he muttered, before he resorted to banging his fist against the splintered wood. 'Mr and Mrs Wilson?' he called in his official inspector's voice.

Inside the flat the voices of the man and woman suddenly died away.

Carly leaned in towards the door and listened. It sounded as if someone was dragging the dog nearest to the door down a passageway. She heard it snarl and growl, then yelp as the man swore again and hit out. 'Do something!' she whispered to Steve.

'Answer the door, why don't you!' Hoody stared at the peeling brown paint, then quickly sidestepped to try and peer through the dirty curtain. 'This is where they've locked the dogs up!' he told the others. 'I can hear them!'

Sure enough, Carly followed and picked up

the sounds of the terrified dogs whining and jumping up at a locked door.

'Mr and Mrs Wilson?' Steve poked the letterbox with his fingers and shouted through the gap. 'Will you please come out and talk to us? It's about the dogs. You've obviously got problems with them. Let's discuss it. And I also want to interview you about a third greyhound that's been brought into Beech Hill Rescue Centre!'

Silence, except for the pathetic whining of the two dogs. Carly saw the grey curl of cigarette smoke twist out through the letterbox; felt the sharp, burning smell hit the back of her throat. Still the door stayed firmly closed.

'Mr Wilson? Mrs Wilson? The police are already involved. Now, unless you fancy another visit from them, I suggest you open up and discuss this properly!' Steve gave it one last try.

Carly closed her eyes and prayed for them to see reason. She felt the next-door curtains twitch, heard doors further down the walkway open and curious neighbours come out to watch.

'If you talk now, I can help you solve the problem!' Steve called through the letterbox. 'Explain to us how the dogs have ended up like this. If not, we're talking about a criminal prosecution!'

In the silence that followed, the imprisoned dogs came to the window and scratched and pulled at the tattered curtain. Carly and Hoody glimpsed two lean faces, two pairs of frightened eyes.

'You understand, Mr and Mrs Wilson? We'll take you to court over this. You could be facing a fine of five thousand pounds, or even a spell in prison!'

Still no one came. They heard doors slam, voices arguing, then the ugly, crashing sound of the guitar music starting up again.

'We'll charge you with cruelty and deliberate neglect!' Steve insisted, backing off and giving up at last.

Carly glared at the locked door.

'And we've got the proof!' she said, under

her breath. They had Grace recovering in intensive care, eye-witness accounts, help from the police. 'All the proof we need to get you sent to prison like you deserve!'

5

'We'll be back,' Hoody swore. 'Those two Wilsons needn't think they're gonna get away with this!'

He sat on his desk in school next day, the top button of his shirt undone, his school tie pulled loose.

Carly had finally cornered him after the last lesson. He seemed to have spent the whole day avoiding her. As the other kids dashed for their buses and scrambled for the exits, she pinned him down in their tutor-group room. 'What are we going to do about Grace?' she demanded, not knowing what answer she was going to get.

'I haven't forgotten about her. I've been busy thinking,' he protested now. 'The problem is, I don't see any answers. Yes, we'll be back; I'm not saying we won't. But . . .' He shrugged and hoisted his heavy bag on to his shoulder.

'. . . But what then?' Carly filled in the rest of the sentence. 'There's not much point hammering on the door like we did yesterday, is there? The Wilsons would just ignore us again.' She frowned and thought hard.

' Definitely,' Hoody agreed. 'No way would they open that door.'

'What we need is a search warrant,' she joked feebly. Then she pulled herself up short. 'Hey!'

'Uh-oh!' He raised both hands to fend her off. 'If you're thinking what I *think* you're thinking . . . No way!'

'But Grace is a police-assist cruelty case,' she reminded him. 'Why didn't I think of it before? The police are the ones who can get a search warrant to go into the flat!' Carly was ready to rush straight to the police station on the way home.

'Count me out.' Hoody shuffled towards the door.

'Where are you going? Listen, it makes sense to ask the police to pay the Wilsons a visit. Think about it for a minute instead of walking away.' She blocked the doorway and tried to persuade him to go with her. 'This is what happens in a cruelty case if the owners refuse to be interviewed. We have to go to the police and they back us up. Sometimes it's the only way to get anywhere!'

'Fine.' Hoody pushed his bottom lip out and tried to step past her. 'What do you need me for, then?'

'I don't need you!' She flared up and let him past, pursuing him down the empty corridor. 'But I thought you cared about Grace, that's all!'

He ignored her, taking a sharp left turn and disappearing behind a row of metal lockers. Carly watched him go. *Typical. Right, I'll do it myself!* No way was Hoody going to put her off getting the help they needed.

The police station was set back from City Road a few hundred metres from the junction with Beech Hill. A railway line ran down the back. It was built of old-fashioned red bricks with fancy stone archways over the windows and doors. Parked patrol cars surrounded the main entrance and people constantly came and went.

Carly stood on the bottom step gathering her courage. There were uniforms everywhere. For a moment she understood why Hoody had refused to come. What was she doing there, after all? Who would listen to her; she was only a schoolkid.

'Hello there,' a friendly voice said from behind.

Carly turned to greet the same woman police officer who had brought the greyhound into Beech Hill on the Saturday. Without her hat and wearing a navy-blue sweater instead of her jacket, she looked even younger than before.

'How's the dog?' she asked, leading Carly up the broad stone steps.

'We think she's going to be OK. And we found the owners.' She grabbed hold of herself and followed the officer into a big reception area.

'Well done.' The policewoman signed a book which took her off duty at the end of her shift. She chatted with other officers as they passed by. 'So you think you can get them to court without us?' she asked Carly.

'Not exactly.' She explained that the Wilsons had refused to be interviewed and that they now knew there were two more dogs at risk.

'I see.' The young woman raised her eyebrows and glanced across the wide desk at her sergeant. 'Have we got anyone free who could get to work on that cruelty case?' she asked.

The older man puffed out his cheeks. 'And pigs might fly,' he muttered.

'I take it that's a no, Serg?' She shrugged at Carly and tried again. 'Listen, I know we're short-staffed as usual, but these owners need to be taught a lesson. This dog very nearly died!'

'And I've got a case-load as long as my arm.' The sergeant checked a computer screen and shook his head. Then he swung it round for Carly and the young officer to see.

Carly's hopes were sinking fast. The sergeant had a tough face; lined and set into a permanent frown. His neat, grey, stubbly haircut made him look stern. As she glanced at the list of names on the screen, she'd practically given up hope of getting the police to help.

'Hang on. What name did you say for the owners of the dogs?' the woman officer asked, latching on to the screen.

'Jet and Misty Wilson. They live at Beacon Heights.'

She nodded. 'I thought that rang a bell. Look!'

Carly read the line she was pointing to. 'Jet Wilson, 22 Beacon Heights. Driving without due care and attention.' There was a case number, a car registration, a brief description of the accident that had injured James, the spaniel-cross.

'What!' She read it again to make sure. 'Does that mean you're already charging Jet Wilson for running James over?' The little dog was out of intensive care at Beech Hill and recovering from an operation to mend his broken jaw. Now it seemed that the police had made a connection between that accident and the dreadful Jet Wilson.

'We would if we could,' the policewoman explained. 'But it was me who went to the flat to speak to him on, let's see, it must have been Sunday morning. Yesterday was Sunday, wasn't it? Yes, that's right. I told him his car had been seen in a hit-and-run incident, but he denied everything.'

'He had his story ready, did he?' The sergeant sounded as if he'd heard it all before, pressing keys on his keyboard to bring more details onscreen. 'Yep, here we go: Wilson says it can't have been him who was driving the car when the accident happened on the Saturday morning because − surprise, surprise −

someone had nicked the car from him on the Friday night!'

Carly gasped.

The woman police constable shrugged. 'Of course, he hadn't quite got around to reporting that the car was stolen before I made contact with him yesterday, but that's his story and he's sticking to it!'

'No wonder he wouldn't open the door to us when we called!' Carly stammered. An earlier visit from the police must have been more than he could take. And what about the excuse he'd come up with about the stolen car? 'Do you believe him?' she asked.

'Ah, that takes us back to pigs,' the sergeant muttered, wrinkles creasing his face as he clicked the hit-and-run details off the screen.

Carly shook her head in deep puzzlement.

'He means, pigs might fly again!' The woman smiled kindly and led Carly back to the door. 'No, of course we don't believe Jet Wilson, but that's the alibi he came up with.'

'So, is he out of trouble?'

'No. Still deep in it, I would say. But we have

to chase up the stolen vehicle story before we can do anything else. And, like the Serg says, we're short of officers and short of time.'

Carly nodded. 'What about the other greyhounds?' She felt she'd come up against a solid brick wall. But there were still two dogs to be rescued.

'Sorry.' The off-duty police officer gave a helpless sigh. 'They're way down the sergeant's list, like he said.'

Maybe his list, but not mine! But 'Thanks,' Carly said to the kind woman. *The dogs are still at the top of my list!* she said to herself. Police-assist or not, she, Carly Grey, was determined to get them away from Jet Wilson if it was the last thing she did.

'This is Peggy.' Bupinda was showing two people round when Carly arrived home that tea-time. The receptionist had taken the visitors into the kennels to view the animals who were up for adoption.

'She's sweet.' The middle-aged woman, who obviously adored dogs, smiled and nodded at the long-haired mongrel who lay surrounded by her brown, black and fawn pups. 'But it's one of the little ones we'd be interested in.'

Carly hung back until Bupinda had finished this nice part of their job here at the Rescue Centre. *Where is everyone?* she wondered. Surgery was due to start in half an hour and there were no vets or nurses in sight.

'The puppies won't be able to leave their mother for a few weeks yet,' Bupinda explained. 'But I'll take down some details and put you on the list for one from this litter, if you're sure that's what you would like.'

She had to speak above the noise of a dozen other dogs barking and grabbing the visitors' attention.

'How big will they grow?' the man asked doubtfully.

'Difficult to say. Don't go by the size of the mother. It depends on who their father was too.' Bupinda let them look a little while longer. 'Of course, if you choose an adult dog, that's not a problem. You already know if your house and garden are going to be big enough to cope.'

'But the puppies are so sweet!' The woman crouched down for a closer look. As usual, getting people to think straight about the dogs they wanted to adopt was difficult.

They won't always be puppies! Carly thought to herself. But the woman had obviously fallen in love with the cute and playful babies.

'What's in there?' The husband pointed to a closed door across the corridor from the main kennels.

'That's where we keep the segregated animals,' Bupinda explained.

'Are they ill with an infectious disease or something?'

'No. We keep them separate because they're the cruelty cases.'

The man frowned. 'That sounds tough; isolating them like that.'

'It is,' Bupinda admitted. 'We don't like to keep the animals separate, because it's generally bad for them. But we can't leave them on view to the public because those dogs and cats are treated as evidence when the case is eventually brought to court. It's all very hush-hush.' She glanced at her watch. Without being rude, she was indicating that she had other jobs to do.

So the woman chose the puppy she would like and the couple followed Bupinda through to reception, where they would arrange a date in a few weeks' time to come and take the dog home. Gradually the dogs stopped barking. Carly was about to open the kennels and let some out into the yard for exercise, when the closed door opposite opened and her dad and Liz came out.

'It's a bit soon for her to be in here by herself,' Paul Grey was saying, 'but we need the space in intensive care.'

Liz was agreeing. 'It's not as if she needs constant nursing care any more. She should be OK.'

Beyond them, in a smaller area than the main kennel block, Carly saw with a start who they were discussing. 'Is that Grace?' she asked, coming out into the corridor, then brushing past her dad into the segregation unit.

She found the greyhound standing

unsteadily inside a wire kennel. The still-skinny dog would be able to move freely along a five-metre run, she would be warm and well-fed. But she would be alone.

'How long will she have to stay here?' Carly asked, her voice catching in her throat. Grace looked unhappy in her new home. Her head hung low and she carried her tail between her legs as she stood trembling miserably.

Paul joined Carly at the door. 'You know the answer to that,' he said quietly. 'The rule is that she stays here until we get the case to court.'

'It's not fair!' No animal, or human being for that matter, would like being locked up in solitary confinement.

'I know, but it's the law.' He watched as Carly went to stroke the dog and steady her. 'We're governed by very strict rules on these cruelty cases,' he reminded her. 'Look at it this way: Grace here is evidence for the court. We can't tamper with that evidence by breaking the rules and putting her in with the other dogs just so she could have some company. The whole case would collapse if we did!'

'Right.' Carly nodded. She ran her fingers over the greyhound's flat head and down her arched neck. 'And she is looking better, isn't she?'

'Much. Anyway, why aren't you with Hoody and Steve?' her dad asked, suddenly looking at his own watch.

Carly stood up and followed him down the corridor. 'Hoody? What's he doing here?'

'He came in straight after school, still in his uniform, which I must say made him look a lot smarter than his usual scruffy self.' Paul Grey grinned. 'I expect he wanted to check on Grace, but he ran into Steve, who's got some good news. Haven't you seen them?'

She shook her head. 'Where?'

'Try the office.'

Carly set off at a run, then stopped. 'What's the good news?'

'Ask Steve. If you're quick, you'll be able to go with him.' He turned off into a treatment room, leaving her standing in an empty corridor.

So she ran to the office. 'What's this good

news?' she gabbled at the inspector, ignoring Hoody.

'This.' He held up a folded sheet of paper. 'A summons from the Magistrates' court.'

'Who for?'

'Jet and Misty Wilson. The magistrate's clerk decided that your dad's statement and the photographs we took of Grace when she was brought in would be enough to bring the owners to court without me needing to interview them. How about it?' He grinned at her. 'Do you want to help us deliver the summons in person?'

Carly was first out of the door and first to the van, sitting nervously in the passenger seat all the way into town.

'Who said we needed the police, then?' Hoody couldn't resist the dig.

She ignored him again. *At last!* she said to herself over and over. She heard Hoody quiz Steve about the summons, but all she could really think about was getting the dogs away from the Wilsons.

'What if they're not in?' Hoody wanted to know.

'Then we come back when they are.' The inspector wove in and out of the rush-hour traffic.

'How long will it take to get them to court?'

'That depends. A few weeks. There's no way of telling, really.' He drove off the ring road into the Ringways estate and pulled up at the foot of the tower block where the Wilsons lived.

'The police think Jet Wilson was the hit-and-run driver involved in the crash with James, the spaniel-cross.' Carly dropped the news into the conversation.

She heard Steve grunt in surprise and Hoody say, 'Wow!'

They got out, slammed the van doors and sprinted for the lift.

'Out of order,' a passer-by told them as they pressed the buttons.

So they took the stairs two at a time, up to the Wilsons' level, and walked quickly to number 22. Curtains on the balcony opposite twitched as people came to their windows to

peer out. Holding the summons ready, Steve
knocked at the door.

Silence. No loud music, no yelling and
cursing. No dogs barking.

Carly glanced at Hoody's tense face as Steve
knocked again.

'Jet Wilson?' The inspector spoke through
the letterbox. 'Come on, open up!'

'You'll be lucky.' The door of number 24
opened and the old man from The Longboat
came out.

'You saying there's no one in?' Hoody jerked
his head towards the Wilsons' door. 'How do
you know?'

The old man ignored him and spoke to
Steve. 'I reckon they knew you or the police
would be back. Anyhow, you can knock
all day and all night and you won't get an
answer.' He shuffled along the balcony in his
slippers, white bristles on his unshaven chin,
his old grey cardigan hanging open. He poked
a finger at the summons in Steve's hand. 'Why
not shove that through the letterbox and save
yourself the trouble?' he asked.

'Can't do that. I have to deliver it to Mr Wilson in person,' Steve replied.

'Huh.' The old man sniffed and began to shuffle off. 'Waste of time.'

'Why?' Carly ran after him. The flat was so silent and empty that she half-guessed the answer before it came.

'They've done a runner, that's why.' The old man growled back. He'd lost interest, was closing his door in her face. 'Packed up and gone. And good riddance!'

'When?' Hoody had followed Carly down the balcony. He stuck a foot in the old man's door to wedge it open.

'Last night. Middle of the night. A moonlight flit.'

By this time Steve had stopped knocking. He stood back from the door, arms folded, his face grim.

The old man leaned hard on his door to close it.

'What about the dogs?' Carly pleaded. She didn't care about anything else. 'Did they take them with them?'

A shrug, a shake of the head. 'Search me,' the old man growled, finally succeeding in shoving the door tightly shut.

6

For a while, Carly, Hoody and Steve stood aimlessly outside the empty flat.

Down at ground level, people coming home from work banged their doors as they went inside. Wind blew across the courtyard, whirling litter and leaves. Half a dozen TV sets gave out the evening news.

'We could break in,' Hoody suggested. He peered through the tatty net curtain into a dark room with a torn sofa and a low table scattered with beer cans.

'Let me think.' Steve planned the next move. 'If the next-door neighbour is right, and the Wilsons really have left for good, I can't believe that even they would leave the dogs behind.'

'I can.' Carly remembered the condition Grace had been in when they found her. 'We should at least make sure!'

'I don't want to break the lock.' Steve was trying the door, which held fast as he shoved his shoulder against it.

'No need.' As usual, Hoody was doing his own thing. He'd fiddled with the sheet of wood that boarded up the second window to the flat and found that it was loose. After a few seconds he was able to slide it away and show them a gaping hole in the glass. 'We could climb through here.'

Steve nodded. 'OK – but go carefully. We've only got the old man's word for it that the flat is empty.'

'I'm the lightest. Give me a leg up,' Carly said.

As they hoisted her in, she listened but heard nothing. 'It stinks of cigarette smoke,' she told them. 'And it looks like they've cleared out anything that might be worth any money.'

There were no pictures on the walls, no TV, not even a carpet on the floor. Her footsteps sounded hollow as she landed. She went quickly across the room, and along the hallway to the front door. She unlocked it from the inside and let Hoody and Steve in. Together they opened the door into a second room.

'Bedroom,' Hoody said, poking his head into a room opposite. 'Nothing here either.'

'And this is the kitchen.' Steve poked around a small, dirty room with a steel sink, an old fridge and rows of empty shelves. 'See, I was right. They took the dogs with them, like I said.' He was about to turn back into the hallway when Carly came up behind and stopped him.

'Did you hear that?' she asked. It was a small sound; a kind of scratching.

'Sounds like rats,' Steve said as he too heard the noise.

Carly shuddered. 'It's coming from that broom cupboard beside the sink.'

'Sounds bigger than rats.' Hoody joined them in the kitchen. He went straight across to the cupboard to investigate.

'No, don't open it!' Carly needed to steel herself. She pictured squat, heavy grey rats with thick tails and sharp teeth jumping out of the dark cupboard on to the filthy kitchen floor.

The sound of their voices made the movements inside the cupboard louder, more frantic. There was a high whine, the scrabbling of claws against the double doors.

'Dogs!' Carly and Hoody said together. They tugged at the handles, found the doors locked, then began to wrench with all their might.

'Stand back.' Steve had found a sturdy knife sharpener inside an open drawer. He slotted it through the handles and levered hard. There was a sound of wood splitting and cracking. The sharpener clattered to the floor and the doors swung open.

Carly cried out and put a hand to her mouth. There inside the shallow broom cupboard were the two greyhounds. Cooped up and tethered all day to hooks in the wall, they were too weak to move or make any noise. One was black, with a white chest, the other a light fawn colour. But they were both filthy, bruised and covered in sores, cowering in the cramped cupboard.

'Set them free!' she pleaded with Steve.

The dogs were so tightly tied by the neck that the ropes had rubbed the flesh raw. Any movement they'd tried to make had made it worse, so that now, starving and exhausted, they could only cower and quiver in the sudden daylight.

Hoody ran to the drawer and looked for a knife, but the inspector quickly took a penknife from his pocket and hacked at the thick ropes.

'We need stretchers from the van!' Steve ordered. He took out his mobile phone and rang Beech Hill to warn them, while Carly came out of the shock of their discovery and ran with Hoody to fetch the stretchers.

'Let's take blankets!' she gasped at Hoody as they flung open the van doors and reached inside. Soon they were racing back up the stairs, lifting the dogs from the floor and wrapping them inside the warm blankets before they laid them gently on the stretchers.

'Ssh!' Carly laid a hand on the black dog's neck. He was trying to resist, but had no strength. The fawn dog, a female, lay quietly accepting their help. Her enormous dark eyes stared from a pale cream face, her thin body hidden now by the thick red blanket.

'We didn't need any more proof, but we got it anyway,' Steve said grimly. He managed one stretcher by himself and told Carly and Hoody to lift the other. 'This is about as bad as it gets,' he muttered, as they made their way out through the front door and along the balcony. 'I've never come across a case like this. Not one, but three dogs in this condition!'

'Watch out, please!' Carly warned the on-lookers who had come out of their flats to stare. They were blocking the head of the stairway, jostling to get a closer look at the stretchers.

Slowly they gave way.

'It's a major case,' Steve insisted through gritted teeth. He pushed his way through the knot of people as they tried to close in again.

'We need to make a big deal of this one; let everyone know that they can't get away with abusing animals like this. If it was up to me, I'd put this pair of monsters away for years!'

Carly had never seen Steve so angry. She caught Hoody's eye as they crossed the courtyard and reached the rescue van.

'He's right,' Hoody murmured, unable to say any more. He looked away, climbed into the back of the van and crouched between the two stretchers.

'But how?' Carly's exasperation broke through. She jumped into the passenger seat as Steve started the engine for the emergency dash to the Rescue Centre. 'How do we get this cruelty case to court if we can't find the culprits?'

'The first job is to get these two dogs back on their feet!' Paul Grey insisted.

He'd called Liz into the operating room to help link them up to drips and examine them.

'The bitch is in a bad way,' Liz reported, sounding the dog's chest with her stethoscope.

She reached for the oxygen trolley and strapped a mask around the animal's face.

Carly stood to one side with Hoody, hoping and praying that they'd got to the greyhounds in time.

'I can't stand this!' Hoody muttered. The tubes and drips, the masks and cylinders, were too much for him. Quickly he turned and swung out through the doors.

'This one's not too bad.' Paul was working hard on the black dog, checking his limbs for fractures, satisfied that the heartbeat was strong, the pulse stable. 'Look after him. Mel, while I give Liz a hand.'

The nurse took over at one treatment table, swabbing at the open sore on the black dog's neck while Carly's dad helped attach small electrodes to the chest of the weaker animal. He glanced anxiously at a nearby screen, then shook his head. 'You're right; she's not good.'

'Do something!' Carly breathed. The dog's big, dark eyes were half-closed, her emaciated body absolutely still except for the painful heaving of her chest.

Liz took another reading. 'Blood pressure's dangerously low!'

'Definitely critical.' Paul Grey assessed all the signs. 'Feel the abdomen,' he told Liz. 'There's a swelling just above the small intestine; could be a ruptured duodenum or pancreas.'

The assistant vet ran her hands along the dog's flank, examining her, and nodded. 'What do you think? Do we take a look?'

He frowned. 'I'm not sure she's strong enough to take the anaesthetic.' It was the same problem as they'd had when Grace was brought in. 'But if we do nothing in this case, I don't think she'll make it.'

Do it! Carly willed them to go ahead and give the dog a chance.

'Let's try,' Liz decided. 'We can at least relieve the pressure from any internal bleeding if we get in there.'

'Have you finished over there?' Paul asked Mel. He went to scrub up at the sink. 'Set up for a blood transfusion,' he instructed. 'And stand by with extra anaesthetic. This could be a long op, depending on what we find.'

Carly watched the two vets and the nurse finish scrubbing up and put on their surgical masks and gloves. Mel wheeled a trolley loaded with sterile instruments into position. Her dad checked the monitors, ready to begin.

'Blood pressure's still falling!' Liz warned.

Hurry! Carly felt the tight knot of anxiety grow inside her chest as the dog disappeared beneath a green screen of surgical sheets.

' . . . Still falling!' Liz repeated.

'More oxygen!' Paul Grey stood poised, scalpel in hand.

Mel turned up the supply of gas from the cylinder.

'We're losing her pulse!' Liz glanced across at Carly, then back at the monitors by the operating table.

'OK, she's crashed. Let's try to resuscitate!' Immediately Paul began to massage the dog's chest, giving more rapid instructions as they worked.

Please! Carly prayed. She saw the jagged line on the main monitor go flat, heard the long, unbroken beep of the machine.

'No good.' Paul Grey let his shoulders sag, then stood back. He pulled the mask from his face. 'Too little, too late,' he said in a quiet, defeated voice.

They called the black dog Arrow. After three days they took him out of intensive care to share the segregated kennel with Grace.

'At least now she'll have some company,' Paul Grey told Carly. He kept a careful eye on the reunion between the two greyhounds.

Grace trotted up to the door of her kennel, carrying her tail level. The tip curved and waved in a friendly fashion. By now the bandage was off her leg and flesh was beginning to form around her ribcage. She no longer looked like the bruised and battered specimen that the police officer had brought in the Saturday before.

Arrow waited until she pressed her long nose against the wire-mesh door. He sniffed, raised his head and wagged his tail.

'They're friends.' Carly sighed with relief.

After the shock of losing the fawn dog, she wanted the two that were left to get on well. 'It's a shame Hoody and I can't take them for walks,' she added.

'No, Carly!' Her dad was definite. 'No walks, no visits from the public. I'm sorry, love, but that's the way it is until the case gets to court.'

'*If!*' She reminded him that since Sunday they hadn't moved forward at all. 'If it gets to court!'

No sign of the Wilsons; full stop. The flat was still deserted, the summons still in Steve's pocket.

'They're bound to show up sooner or later.' Her dad insisted on looking on the bright side. 'People don't just disappear. Do you know if they have any family nearby, for instance? There might be a brother or a sister; someone who could give us a clue.'

Carly nodded. 'I suppose.' For the first time a different thought struck her. 'Dad, what will happen to Grace and Arrow if we never trace the Wilsons?'

He shook his head. 'We will, don't worry.

Once Steve's got his teeth into something, he doesn't let go.'

'No, but if we don't? How long will we keep them as evidence?' She wanted to know how many weeks the greyhounds would have to be kept in isolation.

'Until Steve and the police decide to drop the case.'

'But then the Wilsons would get away with it!'

He nodded. 'I'm afraid so. But at least we could start looking for new owners.' He studied the two dogs, then opened the kennel door to let Arrow in. 'I can't think of many more deserving cases, can you?'

'Will anyone want them?' Before she could stop to think, Carly let slip the unanswerable question.

'Why not? Greyhounds have a lovely temperament. They're gentle and loving, though they do have this habit of chasing everything that moves!' He grinned. 'Stop worrying, Carly. There's a long way to go before we get that far. Let Steve do his investigation first and meanwhile we'll concentrate on getting them back to full health.'

She had to be satisfied with this. But when she saw Hoody in school next day, he was fired up with a new idea for finding Jet and Misty Wilson. After a week of practically ignoring her, he came rushing up to her the moment she arrived.

'I've got it!' He flung his heavy bag at her feet and blocked her way in the corridor. 'It makes sense; listen!'

'What, Hoody? What makes sense?' She was tired. She hadn't slept much lately; not since the dog had died on the operating table. Hoody had been cutting her dead for days, and now he was practically jumping on her.

'Racetrack!' he yelled.

Other kids gave him strange looks as they passed.

'What do you mean, racetrack?'

'Greyhounds. Racing. That's what the Wilsons are into, isn't it?'

Carly remembered the old man who lived at number 24 saying this. She nodded. 'They were there when the police called about the noise.'

'And even if they've done a runner and they don't want anyone to find out where they are, that doesn't mean they're going to stop going to the races, does it?' He spread his arms and laid his palms flat; a gesture that was meant to show how obvious his idea was when you thought about it.

Carly noticed her friends, Cleo and Hannah, stop casually nearby. They listened and nudged each other as Hoody went on.

'How about it, then?' he persisted.

'I don't know.' She shuffled sideways, red with embarrassment.

'Come on, Carly; say yes!'

'I don't know!' she hissed again. She wondered what use it would be just turning up at the greyhound races amongst a crowd of hundreds, or probably thousands.

'Say yes!' Cleo giggled, elbowing Hannah again.

Carly glared at them. 'Maybe,' she told Hoody.

'Meet me at Fiveways at six tomorrow night.' He wanted a definite answer. 'I'll be there anyway. If you don't show up, I'll know you couldn't care less!'

She watched him turn on his heel and storm off. 'It's not what you think!' she told Cleo and Hannah.

'Oh, no!' they chorused. They went off smirking.

OK, Carly said to herself. *I'll be there*. Hoody's idea was better than nothing, as it turned out.

But she wished he'd chosen a better time to ask. All day, everywhere she went, to biology and then to French, she had people whispering in corners and saying the name Hoody out loud to make her blush. 'Carly Grey's going out with Hoody tomorrow night!' The rumour spread like wildfire, and nothing she could say about Grace and Arrow made the slightest bit of difference to what people wanted to think.

7

'Have you ever been to a race meeting before?' Carly asked Hoody under her breath. Everything was strange: the bright floodlights, the people in white coats parading the runners in front of the crowded stand, the dogs looking fit and eager.

Hoody shrugged. 'No. So?'

'Nothing. I just didn't know what to expect.' It was noisier, busier than she'd imagined. Information about dogs' pedigrees, trainers and owners came over the speakers.

They ran the hare around the track before the start of each race; then, as it shot by the traps, the doors flew open and the dogs bolted out in a bunch at full gallop. Shouts from the crowd egged them on, round the vast track in their numbered waistcoats. They strung out as the leaders forged ahead. The lights glared down on them, the crowd cheered as the winner breasted the winning-tape.

The dogs never seemed to discover that the hare they'd been chasing was a fake. Instead, as the hare rattled off the track down a side alley, the people in the white coats came running with leads and led them off, ready for the next race to start.

'It looks like they enjoy it,' Hoody said, sounding as surprised as Carly felt. 'Mad!'

'The mad ones are over there.' She pointed to the sight of people crowding round the betting booths to bet money on their chosen dogs.

'Anyway, if it was cruel it wouldn't be allowed,' Hoody went on. He chewed his lip, staring round the grandstand for a glimpse of two figures in leather-jackets; a man and a woman in their twenties.

After the raid on the flat, the police had given Steve a good description of the Wilsons. 'He's 25 years old; tallish, maybe one-eighty centimetres, and thin. Clean-shaven. Long dark hair tied back. Big nose; that's his distinguishing feature. Apart from the jacket with the motif on the back. It's some kind of bird, an eagle or a hawk. She wears an identical jacket.' The woman police officer who'd been involved in the case from the start had been eager to help.

'What does she look like?' Steve had asked. He and Carly had gone along to the police station to report Jet and Misty Wilson's disappearance.

'About the same age. Shorter, stockier, with dark red hair; dyed and cut short on top, longer at the back. Wears lots of earrings.'

Armed with these descriptions Carly and Hoody had come along to the greyhound track full of confidence. But they'd been there half an hour, seen hundreds of leather-jackets, dozens of men with ponytails and women with dyed red hair. None of them had been in a couple and none of them were the right age, weight or height. Now they were beginning to lose hope of *ever* picking the Wilsons out of the crowd.

'It's not cruel.' Carly carried on studying the crowd between races and agreed with Hoody. 'This is what greyhounds are bred to do: chase their prey and hunt them down. And there's strict rules about how the dogs are trained and treated. That's what Steve's doing here tonight as a matter of fact; checking the conditions in the kennels.' The inspector had given Carly and Hoody a lift across to the stadium, then left them to watch the races while he did his work.

'Pity he isn't allowed to follow up what happens to the dogs once they stop racing,' Hoody grumbled. 'If he was, Jet Wilson would never have got away with starving and beating his dogs.'

This was something else they'd found out since they'd arrived at the track. They'd still been with Steve when he'd asked the course steward if he knew the Wilsons.

The man had frowned and nodded. 'Worse luck.'

'Why?' Carly had stepped in with some quick-fire questions. 'Why "worse luck"?'

'Everyone round here knows them,' the steward had explained. 'They're big gamblers. They might win quite a bit on the first few races, but then they lose it all by the end of the night.

'They fancy themselves as owners too. So what they do is buy an old dog from one of the reputable owners with proper kennels and trainers and so on. They think they can squeeze a few more races out of the dog before it gets too old, but really the dog is ready for retirement. It has no chance of winning any more races, but the Wilsons still reckon they can force a few more laps out of it.'

'Can't you stop them?' Carly had protested. Now she saw why the Wilsons had crowded three racing dogs into their filthy flat.

The man who ran the racetrack had

shrugged. 'It's their money they're wasting on buying the animals and entering them into races. And you try telling them they've got no chance of getting anywhere. They're not the sort to take advice, I can tell you!'

It had made grim listening.

'Are they here tonight?' Hoody had demanded one last piece of information from the steward.

The man had checked his list of entrants into the races. 'Not as owners,' he'd told them. 'But I'd be willing to bet they're here anyway. They never miss a meeting.'

So Carly and Hoody had kept their eyes peeled, scanning the rows of spectators and the queues of people at the betting booths.

'We could ask around,' Hoody suggested now. They were already halfway through the programme of races and there was still no sighting of the two cruel owners.

'Ask who?' Carly looked helplessly round the crowd of several thousand people.

'The people who take the bets.' He led the way down the steps of the stand to ground level and the betting queues. He pushed his way to the front of one. 'Do you know Jet Wilson?' he asked the cashier. 'Have you seen him tonight?'

'Who wants to know?' came the suspicious reply, while people in the queue grumbled for Hoody to get out of the way.

It was the same in the second queue, then the third. Carly had begun to tug at Hoody's arm, telling him they were getting nowhere, when one of the cashiers stopped taking money for a few seconds.

'As a matter of fact, I have seen him,' the woman said quietly. She was young, with short fair hair and dressed in the red uniform of the tote workers. 'Both him and his wife. They were here in this queue about five minutes ago. Why?'

'Where did they go after that?' Carly asked.

'Get a move on up there!' a man in the queue complained. The next race was due to start and he wanted to lay his bet.

The woman went on with her job. 'Don't know. But they put money on a dog in this next race, so chances are they'll be somewhere at the front of the crowd. They don't usually sit in the grandstand. They like to stand round the far side of the track.'

'Thanks!' Carly took a deep breath and together with Hoody began to make her way out of the dense crowd, around the rim of the racetrack in what could be a breakthrough. 'Fingers crossed!' she muttered, aware now that the dogs for the next race were being led into their traps. She saw the hare rattle past on its trial lap, heard the gates fly open and saw the dogs hurtle out.

'Look!' Suddenly Hoody caught Carly's arm and dragged her to a standstill. He stood on tiptoe, pointing over the heads of the crowd.

Carly was smaller than Hoody. All she could see was the outline of heads, the glare of the lights above.

'Stand up here!' He pulled her on to a concrete ledge. 'See, over there! It's them!'

And now she could see. She shielded her eyes with one hand and made out two figures slightly apart from a knot of spectators round the curve of the track. They were wearing leather-jackets. The man was tall and thin, the woman smaller. And when they turned their backs to Carly and Hoody, following the direction of the speeding dogs, there on the backs of their jackets, glowing white in the dazzle of the floodlights, were two birds with wings outspread.

'Come on!' Carly jumped down and began to shove through the thinning crowd towards the couple.

'Wait! What are we gonna do?' Now that they'd spotted them, Hoody needed a plan.

She stopped. 'OK, you're right! Let's tell Steve!' She turned, then stopped again. 'What if we lose them?'

'I'll stay here and keep watch. You fetch Steve!'

'Don't let them out of your sight!' She was off now in the other direction, yelling behind her, but pushing towards the steward's office to look for their inspector. Steve had the warrant with him, she knew. He could come and hand it to the Wilsons in person, make sure they were forced to turn up in court and answer the cruelty case against them.

She heard the crowd cheer the dogs round the last bend of the race, saw the flash of long limbs and lean bodies as the dogs sped by. She ignored everything except finding Steve and hurrying back. In her mind's eye she held the picture of Jet and Misty Wilson leaning against the white rail of the track, craning forward to follow the progress of their chosen dog.

'Too late!' Hoody was angry. He stood in the place where Carly had left him, but it had taken her ten minutes to fetch Steve, and the spot where the Wilsons had stood was empty.

'Where did they go?' Carly cried. She'd been as quick as she could. She'd found Steve in the kennels at the back of the track, talking to the kennel-hands and trainers. The crowd had got in the way as they hurried back, and now Hoody was blaming her for taking too long.

He frowned and kicked at the concrete ledge nearby. 'Their dog lost, I could tell. She was mad with him, started having a go at him. They had this row and stormed off.'

'But which way?' Carly climbed on to the ledge for a better view.

'Out round the far side of the track. I watched them vanish somewhere by that exit. It got too dark to say where exactly.'

Steve heard and nodded. 'Sounds like they'd run out of money,' he decided. 'If they couldn't place any more bets, there wouldn't be any point stopping. I reckon they've given up and gone.'

'And I had to stand here and wait to tell you,' Hoody complained again.

'How long ago?' Carly insisted. She wasn't ready to give up yet. 'How long since they made for the exit?' She got her bearings and worked out where the gate the Wilsons had used might lead.

'Five minutes. They hung around arguing after the race, then she was the one who stormed off. He followed.'

Carly looked at Steve. 'Does that exit lead to the carpark?'

'Yes. It's where we parked when I dropped you off. Are you thinking it's still worth following them?'

She nodded. 'Maybe they have to wait for a bus.'

'Or find their own car and queue to get out.' Hoody decided to stop blaming Carly. He was leading the way round the edge of the track, determined to catch up with the Wilsons.

'They say their car's been stolen, remember.' Carly dodged and swerved past spectators, hearing Steve bring up the rear.

At last they reached the iron gate with the turnstile that led out on to a gravel carpark. The parked cars stood in orderly rows under the orange light of tall lamps, inside a compound that was fenced in by high wire mesh.

'Any sign of them?' Steve clicked through the turnstile behind Hoody and Carly.

Carly saw an old man get into a car by the gate and start his engine. She saw a bus pull away from the kerb on to the road beyond the carpark. 'No.' She shook her head. The road was shiny from recent rain, the pavement empty.

Hoody crunched over the gravel, down the nearest row of cars. He went on looking up and down the deserted rows, but Carly could tell from the slump of his shoulders that he'd given up hope.

She sighed and stopped in the place where Steve had parked the Beech Hill van. Her feet had crunched on something that had a different sound: shattered glass. For a few seconds she stared down at the mess of glittering fragments, then looked up at a gaping hole in the windscreen. 'Steve!' she yelled.

Footsteps came running, but she was still staring at the shattered glass. 'Look what they've done!'

Hoody raced to join them. Out of breath, churning out clouds of steam into the cold night air, they took in what had happened.

'The Wilsons; they must have seen the van and done this!' Carly gasped. 'They're mad with us, Steve, for getting them into trouble about the dogs. Now this is what they've done to get their own back!'

8

'So, we take this as a warning?' Paul Grey said, when he learned about the smashed windscreen. The first thing he'd checked was whether or not Carly and Hoody were OK. He'd called to collect them from the racetrack, and now he stood watching the repair man chiselling the fragments of glass from the rim of the front window frame.

'It's the sort of thing someone like Jet Wilson would do,' Steve agreed. 'He'd see our logo and name on the side of the van and he'd decided it was all our fault. He'd blame us for them having to leave their flat, and for everything else that's gone wrong for them in the last few weeks.' The inspector gave a wry grin. 'He'd probably even blame us for making him back the wrong dogs tonight.'

'Well, I'm not bothered about the van,' Carly's dad said. 'After all, it's only a lump of metal. It's what happens if people get in Jet Wilson's line of vision; that's what worries me.' He glanced anxiously at Carly and Hoody.

She got the message. 'Don't worry, Dad. We'll keep out of his way from now on.'

Hoody said nothing. All the way back to Beech Hill in Paul Grey's car, he stayed quiet. Then, when he was dropped off on the corner of Beacon Street, where he and Vinny lived with his sister, Zoe, and her boyfriend, Dean, he arranged to come to the Rescue Centre to help in the kennels on the Sunday morning.

'Don't forget the clocks go back this weekend,' Carly's dad reminded him. 'Short days and long, dark nights, worse luck.'

They said their goodbyes and Carly went home to a mug of hot chocolate in the flat above the Centre, curled up in front of TV with Ruby the Beech Hill cat for company.

When her dad had finished in the kitchen, he came in to join them.

He leaned forward and rested his folded arms along the back of the settee. 'I mean it, Carly,' he said quietly.

'Mmm.' She was engrossed in her favourite hospital programme.

'If we're right, and the Wilsons are the ones who smashed our windscreen, it means that they're pretty unsavoury characters.'

'We already knew that from the way they treated their dogs.' Carly stroked Ruby's soft tortoiseshell fur. She suspected she was in for one of her dad's 'serious' talks.

'Don't worry, I'm not about to launch into one of my talks!'

She widened her eyes and swivelled them at him. 'Mind-reader!'

'I don't need to be. I can tell by the look on your face.' He bent to kiss her cheek. 'I'm only saying, keep out of their way. And tell Hoody as well.'

'Do you think he listens to me?' She was still wide-eyed, with a little grin curling up the corners of her mouth.

'Well no, maybe not. Just tell him I've handed the whole thing over to the police. That should do the trick!'

'You won't see him for dust,' she agreed. 'Do you want to know something, Dad?'

'What?'

'I'm glad, really. I'd rather concentrate on getting Grace and Arrow properly better.'

He nodded. 'When it comes down to it, that's our job – looking after sick animals.'

'And forget about the Wilsons.'

Her dad was relieved as he went downstairs to check on the patients in intensive care. 'That's fine, then. We can leave the detective work to Steve and the police.'

'They're both gaining weight,' Carly told Hoody.

He'd forgotten the warning about the clocks

going back and shown up with Vinny an hour early. Now they stood quietly in the isolation kennel, watching Arrow and Grace eat breakfast.

'What gets me, apart from the fact that anyone could treat them like that, is how come they get over it without any hard feelings?' Hoody let the greyhounds finish eating, then took Vinny off the lead. The sturdy mongrel trotted up to the kennel door to say hello.

'You mean, why aren't they barking at everyone in sight?'

He nodded. 'You'd think they'd hate us all.'

Instead, Arrow was jumping up at the wire mesh, wagging his tail in greeting. Now that he was less thin and the sore on his neck was beginning to heal, they could see what a beautiful, intelligent dog he was. Streamlined from the tip of his pointed nose to his rudder-like tail, his black coat was short and thick, beginning to shine again under Carly's careful grooming routine.

'Animals aren't like people,' Carly murmured. 'They don't bear grudges.'

'Maybe they trust us too much.' Hoody let Arrow nuzzle against his fingertips through the mesh.

'How come?' The idea had never entered her head before.

'Like, we don't deserve it or something. They think we're the leaders and we're not really. We're not worth looking up to. That's what I think.'

Abruptly Hoody turned and called Vinny.

'Where are you off to?' Carly closed the door on the special unit and followed him down the corridor.

'Park,' he muttered, striding ahead. 'See you down there.'

Carly took Peggy for a walk in Beech Hill Park to give the harassed mother dog a rest from her five pups. Ground frost still covered the grassy slopes and wind had torn most of the leaves from the avenue of trees that led from the entrance down to the long, narrow lake. Carly shivered as she let Peggy off the lead.

But the dog loved the space to charge down

the hill. Her feet carved a trail through the frost, her bark rang through the clear air.

Hoody was chucking small stones into the water. He heard Peggy and looked round. Soon Vinny appeared out of some laurel bushes by the shore and the two dogs happily plunged into the lake to chase the stones. Again and again, Hoody whistled for them to look, hurled a stone and yelled for them to fetch. The dogs barked and rushed in, swimming furiously towards the widening ripples where the stone had landed and sunk. They circled the spot, heads showing, invisible legs paddling. Then Hoody called them back. They swam and waded ashore.

'They look like drowned rats!' Carly laughed.

'They love it!' He got ready to throw again.

Vinny and Peggy shook the water from their coats, all over Hoody.

'Hey!'

'Serves you right!' She was glad they were all back in a good mood, ready to return to the Rescue Centre and bring out a couple more dogs for their morning exercise.

'Race you,' Hoody said, giving himself a five-metre start up the hill.

'Hey!' It was her turn to yell. But she was a fast runner and determined to catch up.

'Come on, Peg. Come on, Vin!' He called the two wet dogs out of the park.

The dogs set off from the lake at an easy run. Within seconds they'd overtaken both Carly and Hoody.

'Tell them to wait at the gate,' she gasped, remembering too late that she ought to have put Peggy back on the lead. Her legs were beginning to tire, though the dogs bounded along effortlessly.

'It's OK, Vinny knows what to do.' Hoody had trained his dog never to run into the road. And Vinny knew the stretch of Beech Hill inside out; the steep rise from the park gates, the pedestrian crossing to the far side.

But Peggy was a stranger to the road. And she was excited by her sudden taste of freedom. Instead of stopping to wait with Vinny by the stone gateposts at the park exit, the corgi- and collie-cross kept going. She was over the kerb and on the crossing before Carly and Hoody could stop her. Vinny barked. A car appeared round the roundabout at the bottom of the hill and came roaring up.

'Watch out!' Hoody waved both arms in the air and yelled at the driver.

The windows were open, loud music blasted out. The man behind the wheel of the battered old car seemed to ignore the warning. He kept on coming.

'Peggy!' Carly cried.

The dog heard the roar of the car engine, must have seen the wheels and the rusty metal grille. She froze in the middle of the crossing.

'Stop! Stop!' Hoody stepped out on to the first white stripe.

Carly realised that the driver didn't intend to do any such thing. She caught a glimpse of a skinny figure with a ponytail; the side view of a man with a thin face and a large nose.

At the last split second, as the car bore down, Peggy unfroze. She leaped sideways, back towards the kerb. The driver swung towards her, but she was too quick. She escaped.

The car tyres squealed, and the driver flashed them an angry look. He stared straight at them, a sneer curling his lip. He swore, then drove on.

'Get the number!' Hoody hissed, stooping to catch Peggy by the collar as she flew to safety.

Carly memorised it. The run of letters on the number plate read 'PET'. Easy; stupidly, mind-bendingly easy.

Hoody held Peggy, who trembled and whined with shock. 'It's OK. It was a narrow escape, but you're OK!' he insisted. 'What was he playing at?' he fumed.

She took a deep breath, repeating the car number to herself. 'Didn't you see who it was?'

He shook his head. 'I know he thought it was all a big joke!' He remembered the sneer, and the way the car had swerved deliberately towards the frightened dog.

'Hoody, it was Jet Wilson!' she cried. 'First he smashes up our van – now he tries to run over one of our dogs!'

Hoody listened and went pale with anger.

He put Peggy on the lead. Vinny had come to heel where they stood and waited patiently. 'I might have known!'

'What's he up to?' Echoes of the squealing tyres still rang in her ears, though the car had vanished up the hill on to the main road.

'He's threatening us.' Quiet and pale, hardly opening his lips to speak, Hoody had it all figured out. 'He's dangerous, Carly. He's the type who gets a kick out of it.'

'Would he have killed Peggy?' Her own voice had dropped to a whisper.

'Without even thinking about it.'

She swallowed. Taking Peggy's lead from him, she set off up the hill. 'Let's tell the police.'

This time, Hoody didn't object. He followed her in silence past the Rescue Centre, to City Road and the police station.

'The registration number ties in with the hit-and-run driver who ran over the spaniel-cross.' The old sergeant was on duty. He checked the computer record of the unsolved case. 'It's registered with Jet Wilson,' he confirmed.

Carly had clung on to the number in her memory, all the way to the police station. 'But Jet Wilson claimed his car had been stolen!' she reminded them.

'So how come he's still driving it?' Hoody spoke up. He pressed his hands against the high desk until his knuckles turned white.

The sergeant clicked the details off the computer screen and pushed out his bottom lip. 'Like I said at the time, it all seemed a bit too convenient. Wilson's car is identified as having been involved in an accident, and what does he tell us when we investigate? Why, he can't have been the driver at the time because the vehicle was no longer in his possession!'

'So it *was* him who ran James over!' Carly claimed. 'That stuff about the car being stolen was a complete lie! He's mad, and he's got it in for us!' She willed the sergeant to come on to their side. 'He is, honestly. Look, he's smashed our van and he's tried to run us over.'

'Hang on a minute; you're not saying that Wilson drove his car at *you*, are you? I thought he drove it at the dog.' The policeman wanted to get the facts straight. He frowned at Peggy, who was still shivering and dripping dirty pondwater over his clean station floor.

'It was. But if it hadn't been Peggy on the crossing – if it had been one of us instead – I'm sure he'd have done the same!' She remembered how the car engine had roared from a dawdling start, had appeared on the roundabout at exactly the moment when they'd all come running out of the park. 'I think he was lying in wait for us!'

'You could be right,' the policeman admitted.

'Now will you help us?' Carly desperately needed him to give the case some time.

'I suppose I could always spare an officer to go and check on the Wilsons' old flat.' He wrinkled his nose and sniffed at the trembling victim.

Obviously not a dog lover, Carly thought.

Hoody nodded. 'And the greyhound track.' He told him about the last sighting of the couple there.

'Trouble is, I'm short of time for a job like this. It's animals, you see. I know the cruelty angle bothers you two kids, but the fact is, dogs are way down the list when you compare them with crimes against people and property.'

Carly felt Hoody stiffen. She jabbed him in the ribs to keep him quiet. This situation demanded them both to be tactful. 'We know that. But in a way it's spilling over into more serious crimes,' she pointed out.

The sergeant nodded. 'You're right. Jet Wilson has overstepped the mark.'

'So you'll send officers out on the case?'

'I don't know about *officers*, plural.' He steadied her down again, then collared a different constable to the one they'd worked with before. 'But I will put Mark here on to it. His car is patrolling the Ringways estate tonight. I'll tell him to pay a visit to number 22.'

'Again?' The young officer overheard and came up to the desk with a sigh. 'I thought the occupants had left in a hurry?'

Carly and Hoody had to be content with this. They heard the sergeant give instructions to the officer on patrol, thanked him, then backed away.

'He needn't have sounded so keen!' Hoody muttered sarcastically on the top step of the station.

'I know.' Carly's head hurt, as if she'd been banging it against a brick wall. 'But at least they're working on it for us. Now there's some hope that they'll find the Wilsons and help us take them to court.'

'Let's get Peggy back inside where it's warm.' He set off up the street.

'Thank heavens it's Sunday; no surgery!' she said wearily. 'There won't be many people around.'

She was right: when they arrived at Beech Hill, the place was deserted. Paul Grey had left the door off the latch and a message for Carly saying that he'd gone out on an emergency visit and that Liz would be in at eleven o'clock to cover for him. It was ten to. The clock above the reception desk clicked forward as Carly read the note. Hoody left Vinny with her, then walked Peggy through to the kennels.

'That's funny!'

She heard him mumble something from

down the corridor. His voice made her click into action. It sounded like he meant 'funny-odd-and-upsetting', not 'funny-ha-ha'.

'Shouldn't this door be kept closed?' he asked, standing with Peggy outside the entrance to the isolation unit.

'Yep. All the time.' She frowned. Why did the room sound so quiet? Were Grace and Arrow both asleep?

She stepped inside.

The secure kennel door where the two greyhounds were kept had been forced open. It swung on its hinges in a draught from the open window. Carly glanced up. No, the window wasn't just open; it had been smashed and someone had climbed through. The same someone had forced open the kennel door and taken the dogs.

'They've gone!' she whispered.

'What do you mean, gone?' Hoody came up behind her. 'They can't be!'

'See for yourself.'

The kennel was empty, there was glass on the floor, but no sign of any struggle.

'Someone's broken in! Hoody, they've stolen Grace and Arrow!'

9

'But they were our proof!' Carly cried. She couldn't believe that the kennel was empty, that Grace and Arrow were gone.

'Calm down.' Liz Hutchins had arrived at Beech Hill to find it in chaos. Hoody was tearing in and out of every room, checking to see if there could be some mistake, still hoping to find the two greyhounds hiding in a corner.

Carly stood in the isolation unit with Peggy and Vinny, too stunned to move.

'Let's think what to do next,' Liz insisted.

'Living proof!' Carly whispered, staring at the empty kennel. 'Without them, we'll never get the Wilsons to court!' Their cruelty case would collapse, the criminals would get off scot-free.

'Never mind about that.' Hoody came back breathless from his search. 'I don't rate the dogs' chances of a decent life now that Wilson's got his hands on them again!'

'Slow down!' Liz protested. 'Are we one hundred per cent sure it's Jet Wilson who's done this?'

They told her about the near accident outside the park. 'He must have driven straight up here, broken in through the back door when no one was here and grabbed them,' Hoody decided.

'His luck was in,' Liz nodded and murmured. 'Five minutes earlier and Paul would have been here. Five minutes later and I would have arrived. As it was, there was no one to stop him.'

'That's why he was hanging around by the park,' Hoody guessed. 'He must have cruised round the streets, waiting for his chance. Seeing us on the crossing was a coincidence.'

'And we thought he was lying in wait just to give us another scare.' Carly saw that Wilson's motive had been much more sinister.

'But really, he was waiting to grab the greyhounds back from under our noses,' Hoody cut in.

'Because Arrow and Grace were evidence against him.'

'And he knew you were looking after them until Steve and the police got him to court.' Hoody helped Carly paint the full picture. 'But you know what that means now?'

'More misery for the poor dogs,' she muttered.

'Or worse.' He stared up at the smashed window where Wilson had broken in. 'Figure it out. What do you do with evidence against you if you manage to get hold of it?'

'Hide it.' Carly was afraid that the Wilsons would keep Grace and Arrow trapped in some filthy cupboard or shed again until the fuss died down.

'Destroy it,' Liz said quietly. She frowned at Hoody. 'That's what you mean, isn't it?'

'Get rid of it for good.' There was no point pussyfooting around. He wanted Carly to face facts. 'That's what I'd do if someone was after me.'

'You mean kill them?' She felt the back of her neck prickle as the message got through.

He nodded, refusing to look her in the face.

'But they can't! . . . They won't!' She turned from Hoody to Liz and back again. The idea was too dreadful for words.

'Unless we find them first!' It took Carly only a few seconds to get over the shock. Liz and Hoody were right. They had next to no time to save the two beautiful dogs.

This was a race to the death. On the one hand, there was Jet Wilson, going back to his wife to tell her that the plan had succeeded, deciding now how to get rid of the problem for good. On the other hand, there was the whole Beech Hill team trying to track them down.

'I'll ring Steve,' Liz decided. 'And the police!' She ran to the phone in reception.

'Someone must have seen which way Wilson's car went!' Carly turned to Hoody for help. Sure, the police and Steve were needed now, but they had to act for themselves too. Hoody knew the area: every back street and alleyway, every kid who hung around on street corners. 'Who should we ask?'

He answered with a jerk of his head, setting off with Vinny on their own investigation. Quickly Carly followed.

'Where are you going?' Liz called.

'To ask around!' Carly yelled from the main door.

'Be back here in half an hour!'

Carly heard the worry in Liz's voice and promised. Then she ran to catch up again with Hoody and Vinny.

'Did an old white car just drive past with two greyhounds in the back?' He ran up the hill and asked a bunch of kids on the corner of Beech Hill and City Road.

'Dunno.'

'Never noticed.'

'Why do you wanna know?'

The careless answers drifted back.

'Did it?' Carly insisted. 'Less than quarter of an hour ago. Did anyone notice?'

'A white car?' One of the kids, a girl with long blonde hair tied up on top of her head with a bright pink band, took an interest. 'I saw one; yeah.'

'Which way did it go?' Hoody shot her another question.

'It came out of King Edward's Road on to City Road; slow, like it was just cruising round.' The girl frowned. 'But listen, there weren't any dogs in the car.'

'Sure?'

'Yeah, and it was more than fifteen minutes ago. More like half an hour.'

'Maybe that was before he broke in,' Carly whispered to Hoody.

'Did you know the driver?' Hoody thought fast.

'Not *know* exactly.' The girl had coloured up under her fair hair, was beginning to regret starting the conversation. She tried to back off.

'But you'd seen him before?'

'Maybe.'

'Where?' Carly ignored the stares. All that mattered was squeezing out every drop of information.

'Near where I live.'

'On Morningside?' Hoody knew without having to ask. Beacon Street, where he lived with his sister, backed on to the Morningside Estate of tower blocks and maisonettes.

'Yes, but I never saw him on the estate.' She shrugged and sighed. 'God, I wish I'd never said anything!'

Others in the group were beginning to get at Hoody and Carly. 'What's it all about?' they wanted to know.

Again Carly took no notice. 'Where then?'

'I dunno. Some row of old shops near us, on Canal Road. I saw him park his car there once, that's all.'

The girl had had enough. She stared at Carly, then turned and headed off up the street with her gang.

'It's OK.' Hoody stopped Carly from going after them. 'I know which shops she means. Come on!'

Minutes were ticking by, but now they had a lead. Wilson had been spotted in the area; not just today, but previously. She ran alongside Hoody and Vinny, back down Beech Hill, through the windy underpasses of the big housing estate and out on to Canal Road.

'It's not far along here,' Hoody told her. 'The shops she was on about overlook the canal. Most of them have been boarded up. I think they're gonna knock them down. There they are.' He pointed a hundred metres down the road.

'We might have known Jet Wilson wouldn't be stupid enough to park his car outside there again.' She saw an empty patch of weed and gravel up ahead, with a row of derelict shops behind. The windows were broken or covered by wooden boards, the paintwork peeled, the walls dripped with damp.

They came to a halt and gazed up at the first-storey flats. 'Some of these look like they're still lived in,' Hoody pointed out.

Carly grimaced. She went behind the row of houses, to find a narrow cobbled alleyway running between them and the canal. 'There's no room to drive a car down here!' she called. Perhaps this was a waste of time after all.

But Hoody was still staring at the flats. He walked past one shopfront, then a second, and a third. 'There's a light on up there.' He pointed to a dirty upper window with a bare electric light.

'But no car!' she reminded him.

'No. But look, someone's forced the lock on this shop door.' He pointed to a patch of newly splintered wood on the frame, then put his foot against the door and gave it a kick. It opened wide.

The smell of damp walls and rotting carpet hit Carly as she peered inside. There was nothing to steal from this mouldering, dismal place. 'Why would anyone want to break into an empty shop? It doesn't make sense.'

As their eyes got used to the dark interior, Vinny went sniffing at the crumbling skirting-boards and damp, curled carpets. He came up against a short flight of steps down into what was probably a cellar.

'Doesn't make sense?' Hoody repeated what Carly had said. 'Oh yes, it does!' He went over and tested the cellar door. The handle wouldn't turn, so he leaned close to listen.

'Can you hear anything?' Suddenly she felt her heart pound. *Of course!* She saw now what he was getting at. Suppose the Wilsons were squatting in the condemned building; that theirs was the first-floor room that was still in use. Suppose they needed a safe place to bring the stolen dogs . . .

'Not yet. Ssh!' He strained to catch any noise coming up through the sturdy, panelled door.

Vinny sniffed and scratched. He gave a sharp bark that echoed through the hollow building.

Carly heard the *drip-drip-drip* of a leaking pipe beyond the door. But no answering bark or cry for help came from the hidden basement. Disappointed, she let her shoulders sag and turned away.

10

Carly reached the door and stepped out on to Canal Road. There was a petrol station opposite, and the banks of flats on the Morningside Estate rising up behind. A double-decker bus went by. But there was no sign of Jet Wilson's battered white car anywhere on the almost deserted Sunday street. She sighed and turned to go back into the disused shop.

Out of the corner of her eye she saw the traffic-light change to red, and glimpsed a white car nose out from behind the bus into the outside lane. She turned to read the number plate. 'B617 PET'.

'Hoody!' Carly lunged inside. 'It's them! They're coming!'

Hoody had armed himself with a metal bar which he'd found on the floor amongst a pile of old paint tins, nails and a hammer. He was using it to try and force open the cellar door, but now he swung it round in Carly's face.

She stepped back quickly. 'The Wilsons! I've just seen their car at the traffic-lights!'

He let the iron bar drop with a clang. 'We've gotta hide!'

They scanned the dark room for a good place. There were wrecked shelves hanging from the walls, an old counter big enough to squat behind. So Hoody ordered Vinny to come away from the cellar door and hide. Within seconds, all three had crouched out of sight. Outside on the road, they heard the bus trundle past, then the scrape of metal on the pavement as the Wilsons' car mounted the kerb and came to a stop on the patch of gravel.

'Shh, Vinny!' Carly silenced the growling dog. Two car doors banged. Would Jet and Misty Wilson go straight round the back and use an outside entrance to the upstairs flat? Or would they come into the shop? 'Can you hear anything?' she hissed at Hoody.

'Footsteps!' He caught the crunch of shoes on gravel.

'Have they got Grace and Arrow with them?'

'Shh!' He didn't have any answers; could only crouch and wait to see what happened.

The steps approached the shop door. It swung open. Jet Wilson's voice broke the silence. 'You were the last one out of here. I thought I told you to shut this door tight!'

'I did. Honest.' Misty Wilson sounded on edge.

'Well, you were useless. Anyone could have come wandering in here.' He strode across the room.

'It was a good thing we could lock the cellar door. No one can get down there,' she reassured him.

Crouching behind the counter, hanging on

to Vinny, Carly held her breath. A key turned in a lock.

'And no one can hear a thing, either.' Wilson seemed satisfied that the cellar was secure. His voice faded and his footsteps began to descend the stone stairs.

His wife gave a nervous laugh. 'Brilliant idea to stick them down here, wasn't it?' She followed him, then paused. 'Shall I lock this door after us?'

'No, leave it. This will only take a couple of minutes. What about the food dishes?'

'Here. Have you got the other stuff we need?' Her footsteps trailed down the stairs. Then there was silence.

Hoody stood up straight and stared at the open door. 'Grace and Arrow are definitely down in that cellar!' he hissed.

Carly's heart was in her mouth. 'It sounds like they're taking them something to eat!' There was the talk of food dishes, the rustle of plastic bags as they'd stopped to check that they had everything they needed.

'They're up to something!' He didn't trust

them. 'It sounds like they dumped the dogs in the cellar and then went off in the car for something. Let's go down and see!'

She nodded and they set foot on the cold cellar steps. One step at a time they went down into the damp, stinking basement.

The leaking pipe dripped water on Carly's face and hand, the rough brick walls felt furry and slimy, the air was so stale it caught in the back of her throat. 'Shh, Vinny!' she whispered again, as he set up a low growl.

'This way!' Hoody had reached the bottom and heard voices along a dark, wet corridor. They saw the dim yellow beam of a torch, heard another key turn in a lock.

'Listen!' Carly had recognised the high whine of dogs trapped in a small space as a door opened.

The corridor was pitch-black again. They stumbled into unseen objects, following the direction of the vanished torchlight, as they felt their way along the rough wall.

' . . . Hurry!' Misty Wilson was whispering from inside the hidden room.

Carly and Hoody halted. They heard more rustling of plastic, the rattle of metal dishes and the frantic whining of the dogs.

'Keep cool. What's the rush?' Jet Wilson sneered. 'No one's ever gonna know!'

'Let's get it over with anyway.' The woman seemed to be backing towards the door again. The dim torch beam played on the wall in the corridor.

Carly dragged Hoody flat against the wall.

'Stay back!' Wilson swore at the dogs. 'Misty, shine the light in here, will you!'

The beam strayed back inside the room. Carly and Hoody breathed again.

'Now I can see what I'm doing!' Wilson grunted as he bent over and seemed to scoop food into the dishes.

'How long before it works?' his wife whispered.

'Not long. This is the stuff they use to unblock drains, remember. Once they eat this, that'll be it!'

Poison! Carly gasped. That's where the Wilsons had been: to buy a chemical that would put an end to Grace and Arrow for good.

'Good riddance!' Wilson gloated. 'A dose of this mixed in with the meat and they won't know what hit them!'

'Shall I untie them?'

'In a second.' He grunted again, scraped a fork against the sides of the dishes, then stood up. 'OK, it's ready!'

Carly and Hoody acted in a flash. They let Vinny loose. 'Go!' Hoody cried.

The mongrel barked and leaped forward. Hoody and Carly yelled loudly as they rushed into the room after him.

Misty Wilson screamed and dropped the torch. Before the light fell and rolled out of control, Carly spotted the greyhounds tied to a hook in the wall.

Vinny went for Jet Wilson. Teeth bared, growling from deep in his chest, he launched himself through the dark at the swearing man. They wrestled. Wilson fought Vinny off and flung him to one side. In the struggle, he kicked the poisoned dishes against a wall.

Carly ran to untie Arrow, then Grace. She held tight to their ropes, steered them clear of the spilled food on the floor.

And now Hoody threw his weight behind Vinny. He launched himself at Wilson, avoiding the man's heavy boots as he kicked out. Hoody was quick and agile, Wilson tall and awkward. The man overbalanced and fell with a thud against the wall, as Carly rushed past a stunned Misty Wilson with the two terrified dogs.

'Get out of here!' Hoody yelled. He sat astride his opponent, with Vinny snarling by his side.

Carly made out the doorway and the narrow corridor beyond. She took the dogs out of danger, towards the dim daylight at the top of the cellar stairs.

Below, the struggle continued. Above, away from the nightmare cellar, there was the wail of sirens as a police patrol sent out to search for the Wilsons spotted their car parked outside the derelict shop. Then came the sound of voices calling Carly and Hoody's names, of feet running to help.

* * *

'We got them!' Steve Winter came striding into Beech Hill and slammed an evening newspaper on to Bupinda's desk.

It was the day of the court case, six weeks after the police had arrested Jet and Misty Wilson in the cellar on Canal Road.

Carly seized the paper. She and Hoody had been into court to give evidence. They had heard Steve give his report of the condition the dogs had been in when they were brought into the Rescue Centre; how one of the three had been so badly neglected it had died. But today, the day of the verdict, she'd been forced to go to school.

Her dad had insisted. 'You've done your bit,' he'd told her. 'And it'll only be a lot of boring lawyers arguing. So it's a normal day for you, like any other!'

She and Hoody had been on tenterhooks. He'd come home with her after school and waited for Steve to bring the news. Now, when he strode in, they both jumped off their seats and cheered out loud.

'What did they get?' Bupinda asked. She scanned the article over Carly's shoulder.

'Six months in prison!' Steve couldn't wait for them to read it through. 'And a five thousand pound fine. The maximum punishment!'

Paul, Liz and Mel came out of the treatment rooms to congratulate him.

'Did they ban them from owning dogs in the future?' Paul wanted to know. He squinted quickly at the newspaper picture of Grace, taken by Steve when she'd first arrived. The photograph had formed a major piece of evidence in the case.

'A lifetime ban,' Steve confirmed. 'You know something? I'm only just coming round to believing it myself. We won! It's over. Finished!'

'And surgery's just about to begin!' Paul Grey nodded towards the door, where a short queue had already formed. 'Open up, Mel. Come on, everyone; back to work!'

'Work, work, work,' Carly grumbled.

She and Hoody had fed the cats in the residential unit, then the dogs in the kennels. The last of Peggy's pups had been collected that day and taken off to a new home. The same kind-hearted person had taken pity on Peggy and offered her a home too. Her kennel was empty, awaiting the next stray or welfare case.

'You like it, really.' Hoody stood in the back yard, hosing down the concrete. It was already beginning to get dark. 'You might moan about it, but I don't know what you'd do without all this.' He waved the gushing hose towards the kennel, splattering the wall and catching Vinny by accident.

Carly grinned. 'So?'

'So, stop complaining.'

She was happy; really happy. Days like today, when the Wilsons were punished and dogs were found new homes, made life at Beech Hill the only one she would choose.

'You know what it means now that the court case has finished?' she asked Hoody as they coiled the hose back on to its reel.

'What?' He shrugged and followed her

146

inside. 'Come on, I'm not a mind-reader!'

She went straight to the isolation unit and opened the door. Grace and Arrow greeted them; sleek and strong. Their coats gleamed, their sores and bruises had all healed.

'It means they don't have to be segregated any more,' she told him. 'They can go in with the other dogs!'

And that was a wonderful feeling: to be able to take the two beautiful greyhounds out of the lonely kennel and lead them into the everyday noise and bustle of the Rescue Centre.

Hoody took Arrow, Carly led Grace. The greyhounds went forward with their high-stepping, prancing walk. Their heads were up, necks arched.

They went eagerly amongst the barks and yelps, down between the crowded kennels to the one at the end where Peggy had looked after her pups.

Hoody stroked Arrow and let him off the lead into the kennel. Carly let Grace follow daintily. Then they stood back and watched for a while.

'Carly, could you fetch a fresh stack of towels into treatment room one, please!'

It was her dad's voice on the intercom. She grinned at Hoody again. 'Thanks,' she murmured.

He blushed and shuffled his feet.

One more second to stare happily at Grace and Arrow. Tomorrow, visitors would be able to view them for the first time. They would have read about the case in the paper. Offers of good homes would flow in.

But for now she had to fetch the towels. Then wipe down the tables in the treatment rooms, then mop the floors and disinfect the surfaces . . . Life at Beech Hill stopped for no one. Carly lifted the receiver of a ringing phone and took another call.

Another Hodder Children's book

ANIMAL
ALERT

GRIEVOUS BODILY HARM

Jenny Oldfield

City life moves fast, but so do the staff at Beech Hill Rescue Centre – if there's an animal in danger, they're first on the scene!

Lucky is a cat who doesn't live up to his name. He's been abandoned once in his short life and now he's been returned to Beech Hill after an unsuccessful attempt to house him.

When the vets discover bruising on his body, suspicion points towards Lucky's previous owners. But the family blames a neighbour with a phobia against cats.

Is she really the guilty one? Can Carly and Hoody find out who's hiding the truth about Lucky's cruel injuries?

Another Hodder Children's book

ANIMAL
ALERT

RUNNING WILD

Jenny Oldfield

City life moves fast, but so do the staff at Beech Hill Rescue Centre – if there's an animal in danger, they're first on the scene!

There's a pack of loose dogs roaming out of control in Beech Hill. Carly and Hoody are helping bring the dogs into the centre, but there's one huge dog they can't get near. They manage to track him down to a boarded-up house, where he keeps a patient vigil night after night.

But who is the dog waiting for? Could he have an owner after all?

ANIMAL ALERT SERIES
Jenny Oldfield

0 340 68169 1	Intensive Care	£3.50	❏
0 340 68170 5	Abandoned	£3.50	❏
0 340 68171 3	Killer on the Loose	£3.50	❏
0 340 68172 1	Quarantine	£3.50	❏
0 340 70878 6	Skin and Bone	£3.50	❏
0 340 70869 7	Crash	£3.50	❏
0 340 70873 5	Blind Alley	£3.50	❏
0 340 70874 3	Living Proof	£3.50	❏

HOME FARM TWINS
Jenny Oldfield

66127 5	Speckle The Stray	£3.50	❏
66128 3	Sinbad The Runaway	£3.50	❏
66129 1	Solo The Homeless	£3.50	❏
66130 5	Susie The Orphan	£3.50	❏
66131 3	Spike The Tramp	£3.50	❏
66132 1	Snip and Snap The Truants	£3.50	❏
68990 0	Sunny The Hero	£3.50	❏
68991 9	Socks The Survivor	£3.50	❏
68992 7	Stevie The Rebel	£3.50	❏
68993 5	Samson The Giant	£3.50	❏
69983 3	Sultan The Patient	£3.50	❏
69984 1	Sorrel The Substitute	£3.50	❏
69985 X	Skye The Champion	£3.50	❏

All Hodder Children's books are available at your local bookshop, or can be ordered direct from the publisher. Just tick the titles you would like and complete the details below. Prices and availability are subject to change without prior notice.

Please enclose a cheque or postal order made payable to *Bookpoint Ltd*, and send to: Hodder Children's Books, 39 Milton Park, Abingdon, OXON OX14 4TD, UK.
Email Address: orders@bookpoint.co.uk

If you would prefer to pay by credit card, our call centre team would be delighted to take your order by telephone. Our direct line *01235 400414* (lines open 9.00 am–6.00 pm Monday to Saturday, 24 hour message answering service). Alternatively you can send a fax on *01235 400454*.

TITLE		FIRST NAME		SURNAME	

ADDRESS	

DAYTIME TEL:		POST CODE	

If you would prefer to pay by credit card, please complete:
Please debit my Visa/Access/Diner's Card/American Express (delete as applicable) card no:

Signature .... Expiry Date: ....

If you would NOT like to receive further information on our products please tick the box. ❏

ANIMAL ARK

Lucy Daniels

1	KITTENS IN THE KITCHEN	£3.50	❏
2	PONY IN THE PORCH	£3.50	❏
3	PUPPIES IN THE PANTRY	£3.50	❏
4	GOAT IN THE GARDEN	£3.50	❏
5	HEDGEHOGS IN THE HALL	£3.50	❏
6	BADGER IN THE BASEMENT	£3.50	❏
7	CUB IN THE CUPBOARD	£3.50	❏
8	PIGLET IN A PLAYPEN	£3.50	❏
9	OWL IN THE OFFICE	£3.50	❏
10	LAMB IN THE LAUNDRY	£3.50	❏
11	BUNNIES IN THE BATHROOM	£3.50	❏
12	DONKEY ON THE DOORSTEP	£3.50	❏
13	HAMSTER IN A HAMPER	£3.50	❏
14	GOOSE ON THE LOOSE	£3.50	❏
15	CALF IN THE COTTAGE	£3.50	❏
16	KOALA IN A CRISIS	£3.50	❏
17	WOMBAT IN THE WILD	£3.50	❏
18	ROO ON THE ROCK	£3.50	❏
19	SQUIRRELS IN THE SCHOOL	£3.50	❏
20	GUINEA-PIG IN THE GARAGE	£3.50	❏
21	FAWN IN THE FOREST	£3.50	❏
22	SHETLAND IN THE SHED	£3.50	❏
23	SWAN IN THE SWIM	£3.50	❏
24	LION BY THE LAKE	£3.50	❏
25	ELEPHANTS IN THE EAST	£3.50	❏
26	MONKEYS ON THE MOUNTAIN	£3.50	❏
27	DOG AT THE DOOR	£3.50	❏
28	FOALS IN THE FIELD	£3.50	❏
29	SHEEP AT THE SHOW	£3.50	❏
30	RACOONS ON THE ROOF	£3.50	❏
31	DOLPHIN IN THE DEEP	£3.50	❏
32	BEARS IN THE BARN	£3.50	❏
	SHEEPDOG IN THE SNOW	£3.50	❏
	KITTEN IN THE COLD	£3.50	❏
	FOX IN THE FROST	£3.50	❏
	SEAL ON THE SHORE	£3.50	❏

All Hodder Children's books are available at your local bookshop, or can be ordered direct from the publisher. Just tick the titles you would like and complete the details below. Prices and availability are subject to change without prior notice.

Please enclose a cheque or postal order made payable to *Bookpoint Ltd*, and send to: Hodder Children's Books, 39 Milton Park, Abingdon, OXON OX14 4TD, UK. Email Address: orders@bookpoint.co.uk

If you would prefer to pay by credit card, our call centre team would be delighted to take your order by telephone. Our direct line *01235 400414* (lines open 9.00 am–6.00 pm Monday to Saturday, 24 hour message answering service). Alternatively you can send a fax on *01235 400454*.

TITLE		FIRST NAME		SURNAME	

ADDRESS	
DAYTIME TEL:	POST CODE

If you would prefer to pay by credit card, please complete: Please debit my Visa/Access/Diner's Card/American Express (delete as applicable) card no:

Signature ....

Expiry Date: ....

If you would NOT like to receive further information on our products please tick the box. ☐